I0766956

I SHOP AT LANEY'S

I SHOP AT LANEY'S

JEFF JOHNSON

Radio Lake Press

ALSO BY JEFF JOHNSON

Nonfiction
Tattoo Machine

Fiction
Lucky Supreme
A Long Crazy Burn
The Animals After Midnight
Everything Under The Moon
Knottspeed: A Love Story
Deadbomb Bingo Ray
Dirty Flamingo

Novellas
I Shop At Laney's
Lemonade
Righteous Fortune Cookies

Radio Lake Press
www.radiolakepress.com
I Shop At Laney's

All inquiries should be addressed to editorial@radiolakepress.com.
This is a work of fiction. All the characters and events portrayed in this book are either a product of the author's imagination or are used fictitiously.
Cover design: Louise Scole
Book design: Manfred Wilkins Jr.
Printed in The United States of America
First Edition
978-1-960495-01-3

I

Laney Bozeman hadn't seen another car since he dropped out of the grasslands west of Carrizozo half an hour ago. Radio reception was bad, full of howling static and pops, but he picked up a station rolling through a long block of The Doobie Brothers and Laney considered this a good omen. The long drive from Ruidoso had been filled with solid portents like The Bros. Just east of Ruidoso he'd glanced down into a high, grassy valley of swaying emerald green and the brilliant ribbon of sunlit stream running through it had perfectly aligned with a crack in the windshield. Best of all, when he stopped for supplies at the grocery store in Carrizozo an hour later and they didn't have any food that wasn't processed to the point of being plastic, by some joyous miracle a toothless old woman was selling shredded BBQ pork and green chili tamales out front. Laney bought the entire batch, and she was so pleased she pinched his cheek and gave him the Dollar General Styrofoam cooler she was using for free. He was going to freeze them and eat like the grande rancheros of old for the next two weeks. In the absence of good beer, Laney settled for three plastic bottles of the cheapest whiskey, reasoning that any whiskey at all was better than shit beer. Cheap whiskey paired well with stargazing. It complimented refried tamales and beans with red sauce. The TV in the shabby attendant's bungalow adjacent to The Rock Shack got one station, and a nip of whiskey made that station interesting. Miles passed and as night washed over the desert, Laney's thoughts rambled along to the crackling radio and a block of Bob Seger. Working at The Rock Shack was the best job he'd had in New Mexico, certainly better than anything in Idaho, where he was from. The owner of the isolated place was a hard old ex-Marine named Gant who checked in by phone once a week, and Laney had only seen him twice in the last nine months. For the next two weeks he'd sell imitation arrowheads from Juarez, shiny rocks, ambiguous fossils, and overpriced bottled water to passing motorists, then it was two weeks off, with just enough money in his pocket to bum around doing nothing at all as long as it wasn't expensive. It worked for him. The only people who stopped at The Rock Shack were station waggoneers from Ohio or Michigan, friendly little family units who wanted to use the outdoor toilets and stretch their legs. Mr. Gant wanted Laney to dig in one of the back lots for new stock when it was slow, which was always, but Laney only did shovel work in the mornings, when it was cool and breezy and it felt good to do it. Most days he sat at the register with an old paperback and manned the phone that never rang. It was better than day work in Ruidoso, which was mostly ditch clearing and paid the equivalent of two peanuts and a banana, and it was slightly better than stocking shelves at the grocery store in Santa Fe, the job he had before bumming around Ruidoso.

But all good things, even the lazy and pointless ones, must come to an end. Maria Ortiz worked at Big Donut in Roswell, and she was way out of his league, he knew, a rare and stunning beauty with flowing, lustrous black hair and sparkling eyes. A week ago, she'd shyly asked him if he wanted to eat dinner with her at the all-you-can-eat steak-house buffet, and now they texted back and forth every night. Maria wanted him to meet her parents. She was apprehensive about how they would take to a gringo suitor from Idaho who slept in his truck much of the time, and Laney's description of his current job as a geology craft associate was sure to raise eyebrows.

Laney smiled, thinking about Maria and her tight pink Big Donut tee shirt, her flashing smile and musical laugh, the way she gestured, and her curiously long fingernails. When The Rock Shack finally came into view any thought of enjoying what might be his final two-week shift evaporated. Even from a quarter mile away, it was obvious something was seriously, terribly wrong. All the lights were on, and the place looked like a municipal airport glowing in the night. Laney's jaw clenched and his hands tightened on the wheel.

"Orley," he hissed.

Ralston Orley was a hard-drinking old cowpoke bum he never got along with, and by unspoken agreement, he was to be gone at sunset. Orley always left the attendant's bungalow in a wretched state, so creatively filthy it was like a family of hallucinating raccoons had been nesting inside, and this time Orley hadn't left at all. It was a challenge of some kind. Orley had waited for him this time and it could only mean one thing- the old man felt like losing a fight.

The front gate was open and gently swaying back and forth in the breeze. Orley's rusted old truck was parked sideways in the gravel in front of the bungalow and the driver's door was open. Laney parked in the small parking lot, closed the gate, and stalked to the bungalow with fire in his head. He was an even six feet tall, with sandy hair and blue eyes, dressed in old jeans, a faded western shirt, and worn cowboy boots. He generally had an open face and an easy demeanor, and he wasn't particularly imposing even when he was furious, which he was. The front door to the bungalow was ajar and the light in the window flickered with gray light- Orley was inside, watching TV. Laney picked up speed and kicked the door open. The parade of insults on the tip of his tongue died and his mouth was suddenly as dry as cave dirt.

Ralston Orley was sitting on the tattered green sofa facing the old TV, which flickered on a dead station. He was wearing threadbare underpants, a gun belt with a Colt .45 in the holster, and he only had on one cowboy boot. The toenails on his free foot were spectacularly gnarly. His big gut, normally self-consciously tucked in, hung low and wide in his lap, and his bloodshot eyes were glassy and vacant, ringed with shock and insomnia. There was a mostly empty bottle of vodka and an open can of beans with a spoon sticking out on the rickety TV dinner stand beside him. Worst of all, Orley had dragged a huge piece of metal into the tiny living room. It lay between them, an oddly shaped thing that was worn and pitted with age and about the size of a motel mattress. The floor was scarred with deep grooves marking its passage. Laney took in the entire tableau for a full thirty seconds before he could speak.

"Orley," he whispered fearfully. "What- what the hell is going on here?"

Ralston Orley looked at him and blinked. There was no recognition in his lizard eyes. It occurred to Laney that the boozy old cowboy had finally lost his mind.

"Dude!" Laney yelled in rising panic. "What the hell man!"

Orley opened his mouth to speak. Nothing came out. Laney watched for a long moment, rapt, as the older man tried to form a word, his mouth working around something too difficult to pronounce.

"Talk to me pal," Laney said softly, changing his tact and trying for a sympathy he didn't feel. His best option was to get back in his truck and floor it. He could call Mr. Gant from the road and tell him something. He had no idea how to describe the scene before him.

Somewhere behind Laney, in the immense silence of the desert night, a lone owl let out a haunting steam whistle blast. Orley seemed to respond to the call and stiffened, then abruptly tossed his head back and let out a terrible, drawn crow caw. Laney was frozen in horror as Orley raised one hand and pointed at the huge piece of metal he'd dragged in, and his eyes widened with fresh, suffocating madness as he did. Laney glared down for the span of a heartbeat and then violently lurched back.

The metal object on the floor between them, weathered by uncounted years, was a gigantic belt buckle.

2

It was a long night for Laney Bozeman.

It took two hours to get Orley's gun away from him and then get him in the only bed. In the end, Laney had no choice but to feed him whiskey, sip by choaking sip, until Orley's eyes rolled back and he passed out. After that, Laney aired the house out and cleaned the kitchen and the bathroom. When he was done, he sat down on the front porch and had two fingers of whiskey himself. He was, he knew, unsuited for situations like this. A madman, a giant belt buckle exhumed from the sand, it was all beyond his purview. Laney didn't even know someone who could deal with this kind of thing.

He thought about Maria Ortiz, who was no doubt sleeping peacefully in her little trailer in Roswell. Maria smelled like donuts. Finally, an unstoppable wave of exhaustion washed over him, and Laney went inside and lay down on the couch. He avoided looking at the giant belt buckle. Orley snored and gurgled in the next room. Laney turned out the light and his eyes adjusted to the darkness. The dark out in the desert was different from city darkness, or even the night in Idaho. There was soft starlight in it, and the whitish-blue seemed to seep through the cracks, illuminating everything with a barely visible halo. The giant belt buckle dominated the room. Laney turned its impossible presence over and around in his mind, again and again, until he was so disturbed that he turned the light on.

It looked like a normal buckle, but there was something transcendently sinister about it. Laney had a long-standing superstition

5

regarding belt buckles. The size of a man's belt buckle was a projection of something inside him. The small, utilitarian ones whispered of meekness, or common sense, though sometimes they betrayed a serpentine slyness wrapped in fashion. The big ones told a different tale. A large belt buckle was like a monster truck driven by a man who couldn't work on the engine, or a handlebar mustache on a skinny man with a big mouth and no guts. The larger the buckle, the worse it was. If all that was true, and Laney knew in his heart that it was, then the incredibly massive belt buckle on the living room floor was the very totem of evil.

Laney took his sleeping roll out to his truck, unrolled it in the bed, and climbed in. He could still feel the presence of the buckle, but it was far enough away to relax and think of something else. Laney considered the stars, as he often did when sleeping in the truck. They had individual names, he knew. The North Star, Vega and Aldebaran and Rigel. He didn't know which was which. It was the same with the constellations. He didn't know any of it. All of it was a mystery and it would remain that way for him even if he lived to be a hundred. He enjoyed the night sky better this way. He didn't know the names of the flowers or the trees for the very same reason. Moments passed, and he was finally dozing off when he saw his first shooting star. He made a wish, tossing it to the heavens from the edge of sleep. He wished that Maria would think of him while she was making the donuts in the morning. It was a small wish, so it might sneak by.

An hour after sunrise, Laney woke and went back into the bungalow to make coffee. He didn't look directly at the buckle and he didn't check on Ralston Orley. When the coffee was done, he poured two cups, went into the bedroom and sat one of them beside the bed, then gently prodded Orley with the toe of his boot until the old man woke with a jerk, his eyes wild and lost. Laney carried his coffee out to the porch and leaned against the railing. It was early March, so it wouldn't be too hot or too cold. A few high, gauzy clouds seemed to stand still in the sky. A lone, loud horsefly circled him and lost interest.

Ralston Orley eventually emerged with his coffee. He'd managed to dress in a rumpled, faded western shirt with yellow roses on the chest and plastic pearl buttons, jeans that were so old they were almost dirty white, and he was wearing both of his crusty cowboy boots. Orley lit a cigarette and took a hard drag, coughed wetly and spit over the rail into the hard packed dirt. Laney scowled at him. Orley scowled back and took up station beside him. The railing creaked as he leaned into it and surveyed the horizon through slitted eyes.

"Morning." Orley said it like an observation, not a greeting.

"Yep." Laney squinted at the horizon, too. "So, ah, what's up dude?"

Orley sucked on his cigarette. Laney waited patiently. Eventually, Orley spit again and fixed Laney with a hard gaze. His bloodshot eyes were poison.

"I never like you, Laney," Orley began. He shook his head, scowling, and looked down at the dirt in disgust. "First time we met, right after Gant hired you and you came out with your little box of bullshit Chinese soup and your finger crackers and whatnot, you remember that night?" He glared at Laney again, angry. "You mouthed off about my personal hygiene right in front of the boss and then you carried on about the sink an' the toilet like-"

Orley went on and on, but Laney wasn't really listening. Instead, he was thinking that this was the first time he'd ever seen Ralston Orley in broad daylight, and how perfectly homely the man was. Orley was splay-footed, and with his big gut sucked in he had the lumpy form of a potato grown in rocky ground. The limp, graying hair on his round head was thinning and greasy. The three days worth of hoary stubble on his sallow, pockmarked face looked like wire bristle poking through a rare foreign cheese.

"-told Mr. Gant that it was not the proper way to run a place like this. A kid like you can ruin an establishment like The Rock Shack. You don't even have sales experience, and I mean not even hotdogs or ice cream cones at the fair. It's the attitude that makes or breaks-"

Laney looked at Orley's belt buckle and laughed out loud. It was A Texas Prison Rodeo Commemorative coffee saucer. Orley stopped talking and gave Laney a blistering glare.

"Are you even listening to me, boy?" Orley pushed off the rail and faced Laney. His jaw muscles flared.

Laney scowled and stepped closer, just to illustrate that he was nearly a head taller. "Cut the shit, weirdo. Where the hell did you get that buckle from and why is it in the living room?"

Orley looked briefly confused. Finally, he shrugged and looked back out at the horizon.

"Day before yesterday I was out digging in plot number nine, way up at the north edge. God damn Gant wanted to see progress, kept on callin', so I went out just after sunrise. Hit on a patch of it in the first ten minutes. Dug out the shape and... shit. I couldn't believe my eyes." Orley's voice grew quiet. "S'hard out here, you know that. Not one soul stopped in in the last two weeks, not even to use the porta john. So I went at it, and the more I dug the worse it got. I had it bare just before sunset an' I'd been workin' on it all day, my mind just runnin' an' runnin'..." He trailed off and swallowed.

"You freaked out," Laney offered. Orley nodded.

"Went crazy as hell, son. Like I'd finally lost my mind out here, like all the loneliness and the owls and that big damn sky had come to roost in my head, like all the four dollar whiskey and- I can't describe it. Whole thing kicked me over the edge." He stared into his coffee cup.

"So you dragged it into the living room." Laney nodded. "Good. Very rational."

Orley wheeled on him. "You seen that thing! It can't be, Laney! As in it has no place in the world! That buckle shouldn't exist but there it was, buried in the sand!" He pointed at Laney. "Why'd you sleep in your truck, answer me that? I know you did so don't bother to lie. That buckle scared you, deep down it scared you 'cause you thought the same thing."

"I slept in my truck because there was a hobo in the house and he was drunk tank wasted with a gun on his hip." Laney squared off with him. "And because you smell bad, Orley. You smell like an unplugged refrigerator full of feet. You stink like this pony I shoveled up when I worked a road crew in Idaho. You-"

"You ain't gonna tell me that thing in there didn't spook you, boy." Orley looked like he was ready to swing. "That'd be the wrong kind of lie."

Laney rolled his eyes. "Fine. Fine. It freaked me out. Why didn't you just leave it? I'd have buried it again as soon as I laid eyes on it, and then... Shit. Probably pretended like it never happened."

Orley dialed it back, took a breath and shrugged. "Figured I'd sell it. A thing like that has to be worth something to somebody. Face it, Laney. Neither of us wants to say it, but that buckle in there belonged to a giant from a long, long time ago. Yesterday morning I dragged it with my truck and used a come along to pull it into the house. God damn took forever too. Don't know why I thought somebody would steal it, but that's what I thought all night, didn't sleep a wink. And then once it was inside, well, you saw what happened. Same thing happened to you. I looked and looked, and I got worse and worse in the head. I tried to drink it off like a bad shock, like after a car wreck or somethin', but that just made me nutty as hell." He shrugged. "Now here we are."

Laney laughed bitterly. "You call Mr. Gant?"

"And tell him what?" Orley snorted. "Hi Mr. Gant, it's Ralston Orely out at The Rock Shack. Yeah, so I found this ginormous belt buckle when I was digging for new stock. Made me feel real crazy so I hit the bottle. Dragged it into the bungalow for safe keeping and I messed up the floor in the worst way. Just checkin' in. Sir."

Laney nodded. "I guess that would be bad." He sipped his coffee thoughtfully.

"Yeah."

"So you waited for me." Laney cleared his throat. "Waited for me to come out for my two weeks and find this crazy shit and... What?"

"I forgot all about you." Orley sounded lost again. "I forgot the day of the week. I sorta forgot where I was for a little while." He turned to Laney. "You ever seen the impossible? Even one time in your life before this?"

Laney considered. Orley had a point. "One time in Idaho I was driving home from our high school football game and a deer jumped clear over my truck. I thought that was impossible, I mean when I looked in the rearview and saw it keep on running I almost wrecked. Then one time in San Diego I saw a train miss this guy by a hair, and I mean one hair, and he didn't even notice. He was on his phone, just kept on walking."

"That ain't nothin'." Orley was disgusted. "One time, years back in Oklahoma there was a twister, real bad, I guess that was in '76 or '78. Afterward, I was lookin' through the wreckage thinkin' maybe I'd find something valuable, like a necklace or a blender that made it through whole, and what did I find? Puppy in a toilet, and not a scratch on 'em. Toilet was all chipped, clear as day it had been up there in the clouds a whirlin' an' flyin' but there it was, and there was the pup who rode in it. Looked like he just woke up too, yawned at me and gave them blinky eyes, shit." Orley shook his grizzled head. "And that ain't nothin' compared to findin' that buckle. The mind ain't made for the incomprehensible, least mine ain't. Once I dug it up and I stood back, I-" He searched for the right words. "I felt like Santa was real, the Tooth Fairy and the Boogeyman too. I felt like everything I never believed in was real and I was in a world that was bigger and deeper and way more... huge than I ever thought. My head felt like- like a ringin' bongo. Empty and loud and full of echoes. I dunno." He smiled sadly, a private smile that was just for him. "I still sound crazy."

"Wow man."

Orley nodded.

They were both quiet after that. Orley smoked. Laney finished his coffee and then he just stood there. He was tired, but more than that he was deeply unsettled. Orley was in genuine distress, and Laney understood why. The giant buckle exuded a quality that made it stick in the mind and it was hard to think of anything else. Eventually, Orley cleared his throat.

"Laney, how well you know Gant?"

Laney looked over. "I don't. Why?"

"I had a head start on thinkin' about that buckle. I been workin' here for, oh, goin' on three years now. Before me there was a guy out here name Freddy Tamayo. He was a good ole boy, I think he genuinely liked rocks, too. Now, when I came on, Freddy said he'd been on the payroll for close to five years, and before that Gant himself was out here. Now think about that for a minute. A rich man, living out here and diggin' around in the hot sun. Then he hires Freddy to do it half the time. Now he's got me and you. Now, why is that? We don't make our salary, pitiful as it is, the register just don't ring that often. The Rock Shack is a losing proposition no matter how you look at it. So why the hell is this place really here?"

"You mean you think Mr. Gant knew there was a giant belt buckle out there?" Laney laughed, but now he was suspicious, too.

"I dunno." Orley's eyes narrowed to slits. Thinking was a powerful exercise for him, Laney could tell. "Always with the digging though, more now than ever before. Finish one grid square, start on the next. Finish the last one, start over at the beginning."

Laney began to see where he was going. "What we have here is a mystery."

"That we do."

"Okay. Let's start at the beginning. How'd you meet Mr. Gant?"

Orley thought back. "I was on a landscaping crew in Las Vegas. We dug and poured the little foundations for air conditioner units. Gant, shit, he was livin' out there I guess. Maybe he was visiting a woman, I dunno, but when I knocked off one day, he came around and commented on my work, asked me if I drank beer. Not too friendly, but he asked so I said hell yeah, which was honest. We hit up this local bar and five beers later I had a job." Orley's face bent with bitter reflection. "He put a smiley face on this shit ass gig, too. Said there'd be free franks-n-beans and there was always a house bottle, raise every year if I did my diggin'. Lies. All lies."

"Strange," Laney said quietly. "I was shoveling manure in Ruidoso, right after the Roundup. Gant came around and asked if I'd rather dig in the sand. Had this way about him, like he was a judge lookin' down from the bench and I was some kid who got caught stealing a slushie. I thought he was an asshole and he knew it. When I was done, I walked down to Farley's and there he was. Bought me a round like he was trying to apologize and three beers later he offered me a job."

"Well that don't mean a goddamn thing," Orley said bitterly. "He hired a dimwit shit shoveler and a broke down Vegas air conditioner man."

"What'd you guys talk about? That first night?" Laney could feel they were on the trail of something.

"Family." Orley shrugged. "I ain't got none. Never married 'cause I like wild women who drink and fight, so why the hell would I. Shit like that."

"Gant asked me about family, too. I don't have any either."

Orley glanced over at him. "That's a fucked up thing to have in common. But that's interesting."

"It is," Laney said gravely.

Orley looked off at The Rock Shack. "Here we are. Me and you, two nobodies drifting through the world without a single person who'd notice if they were gone. And we don't get along so we wouldn't even miss each other. Digging and rootin' around day after day in the middle of nowhere. And then one of us finds a giant belt buckle." He pursed his lips. "What else... What else..."

"The digging," Laney said slowly. "He ever tell you to look for anything specific?"

"No." A lightbulb clicked on over Orley's head and he snapped his fingers. "But you remember what he always says. You find something and you don't know what it is, call him on the landline. I always thought he was talking about anything valuable, like the time I thought I found that dinosaur tooth."

"Call right away," Laney nodded. "Told me too, really serious about it."

"New Mexico is the tyrannosaur state." Orley sounded vaguely proud that he knew.

Laney said nothing. It sounded true.

"Gant has that little office room over in the shack behind the register. His little private space for receipts and old maps and probably pictures of his trophy gals." Orley banged his cup on the railing. "I say we break in and take a look." He looked back into the bungalow. The door was open to air the place out, and in the bright light, the damage to the floor was clearly severe. Dragging the giant buckle had left deep, splintery grooves in the old wood, and the door jam itself was cracked. "Already messed up the house. Let's try our hand on the shed."

Laney shook his head. "No man. No. Time to make the rational move here. We take that buckle back out where you found it and bury it again. Then you drive into Ruidoso and get some new boards at the lumber store. We fix the floor, and we never say a thing. This'll make for a fun story years from now and that's about it."

"You scared?" Orley said it with oil and malice. "You are. I knew it."

"Nah." Laney appraised Orley, measuring him. "You don't think you can fix the floor." Laney looked away. "I'll do it. I did the whole roof on a barn last year, this has to be the same kind of fit and hammer. You just get the wood."

"Coward." Orley spit again, a long stringer of bile. "Kids anymore don't have spleen, s'like you were all born with tiny nuts. Gant is a rich man, and he pays us pennies to dig around out here, two bozos with no connections to the outside world, two guys who wouldn't work together or drink together and sure as shit wouldn't trust each other in a million years. Too perfect. I smell a secret. A rich man's secret." Orley poked Laney in the shoulder. "You go on if you want to but I'm runnin' this down."

Orley was right. Reluctantly, Laney nodded. "We should eat breakfast. I got some eggs and a whole shitload of tamales."

"Let's fry it up."

3

The Rock Shack was an old tin-roofed Army bunker with pressed wood and pine walls, forty feet long and twenty feet wide. Running down the center was a row of dusty wooden bins full of geodes and assorted chunks of rock. Plastic windows, now warped and frosted with sandblast, had been set into the wall facing the road. Under the windows was a long bare wood shelf with their prized collection of fool's gold, fake arrowheads, and quartz crystals. The entire back wall was a mounted display of old prospector tools and faded black and white photos of miners that, on close inspection, were cut from National Geographic. Gant's office was in a little room just behind the antique cash register, which was set up on the pocketknife display case. Orley didn't bother to try and pick the office lock. He kicked the door open, splintering the sash, and Laney followed him in.

There was a scarred old oak desk with a chair and two metal file cabinets with three drawers each. Everything was covered in a layer of dust. Orley crossed around to the far side of the desk and crashed down into the chair. A cloud of dust rose around him, and he coughed. Laney tested the file cabinet drawers. Locked.

"Desk drawers are locked too," Orley reported.

"Let's wreck 'em open." Laney went back out into the shack proper and came back with two rusted crowbars. He handed one to Orley and turned his attention to the file cabinets. The lock was on top of each case and they both popped easily. All six drawers were full of old papers. Laney began going through them, searching for anything that might tell them more.

"Ton of receipts," Laney mused. "All from the 1990's. Some pamphlets for UNM science talks. Physics."

"Hmm." Orley moved through the desk more slowly, scrutinizing every item. "Junk. Just a bunch of junk. Gant has three staplers and there ain't a single staple in 'em. All empty." He was quiet for a moment. "Lotta rubber bands."

They worked for a long time in silence and the day slowly wore on into the afternoon. Orley took a long break to refill his flask at one point, and Laney took some time to get the dinner beans started, relieved to get out of the dusty little room for a while. He fried an onion in their big pot, then added salt, a can of chopped tomatoes and a can of water, three cups of dry pinto beans, then set it on low with the lid on. When he went back out to continue it was late afternoon and Orley had nothing to report other than being drunker. By early evening, Laney was up to 1994, and Orley finally got bored enough to start talking.

"I almost got married. Wouldn't be here if I did, I guess. Long time back in Montana. True love an' all that."

"That right." Laney didn't want to hear it.

"Might want to tell a little bit about ourselves, boy. Gant knows more about us than we do about each other. That can't be good."

Laney paused. "So what happened? To your almost wife?" He began working again. He didn't really want to know. Behind him, he heard Orley take a pull off his flask.

"She was magnificent. I was on a tear in Billings. Three months on the pipeline and I finally got paid out and boy, I hit the city with a roll in my pocket and a terrible thirst. First night I was sitting at the bar in this one little shit hole dump, can't remember the name of the place, but that's where I met her. Short, kinda frizzy hair, halter top under her coat and lord she was hell on wheels. Came into the bar loud, like she owned the place or she was famous, and she took one look at me and I took one look at her and it was game on." Orley paused, savoring the memory.

"Billings is a good town for dives," Laney said. He studied a receipt for an oil heater filter and kept going.

"Aw yeah. There were maybe ten people in the place. Couple old boys at the pool table, some old gal with big hair a few stools over, a handful of ground up burnouts scattered at the tables, but even they knew me and that angel were meant for each other, I could see it in their eyes, the way they all looked back and forth between us like they could see an invisible link, like she was the Princess of Bismarck and I was the Duke of Muncie." Orley snorted. "Anyway, five drinks later we went at it like, oh, like Dobermans in a Soviet steroid experiment. Started in the men's room an' moved to the motel and then beyond. Day three I found my truck again and we lit out before the Billings PD brought the hammer down. I loved that truck, too, my goddam little world was full of love right then. 1974 F-250 with an over-the-top camper, little butane stove. Even had a fake bearskin rug I got at the flea market in Fargo. It was run down an' I ain't much of a housekeeper as you know, but it was home. Summer wasn't far away so I pointed us east." Orley's voice got quieter. "Yeah. That was my mistake, lookin' back. Ain't shit in North Dakota, but Watford City has a few good bars and I think that was the plan. Keep the party goin' so hard that it just went on forever, like it would take on a life of its own and wash us along all the way into eternity." The chair creaked as Orley sat back. He took another pull off the flask. Laney paused and listened. There was some new quality in Orley's voice.

"Storm rolled in. I took a side road off the highway, thinking maybe I'd slide south on under it, but it caught us, way out there in the wide open nothin'. We got in the back and cracked a bottle, and I could tell she was scared, poor gal. I was too. The clouds were so huge and so damn black, webs of lightnin' all flashin' between 'em like witch fingers. Air smelled like ozone, and it got so... still, like it was the last hour of the last day of the final century." Orley's voice had gotten even quieter, like he was telling a ghost story around a campfire, and Laney knew he wasn't doing it on purpose. "And then it was on us. The thunder cracked the air itself. Boy, it was like somethin' outta the bible, these long, deep, rollin' booms that shook the roots of my teeth and the bones in my head. I could feel the shape of my spleen for the very first time, vibrating like a robin's egg in my gut along with everything else. Rain came up and then it was like a river of lightning struck the truck. Again and again, light and sound, too bright and too loud to make sense out of. Flashes so bright I swear I saw her skeleton right there in front of me. And it went on. And on. And on. So loud it was like I stuck my head in an airplane engine and so bright and then so black that my eyes broke. I was screamin' and so was she, an' I think we both screamed until there weren't a thing left in either one of us." Orley sniffed. "I passed out at some point, she blacked out too, I don't know how long she held on. When I woke up, shit, it was to a clear blue sky. My barroom angel was out cold, still clutchin' the bottle, her mouth was open like she was about to sing me a tune. I climbed out into the world and I couldn't believe my eyes. All four tires were flat. The antenna and the windshield wipers were all wound up into crazy little balls, never seen anything like it. I looked out across a bright field of mud and corn stub and way in the distance I see a farmer on his tractor. We ain't goin' nowhere with four flats so I started walkin'. I get closer and he finally sees me and boy he stands up and starts wavin' all frantic and I think to myself, good lord, even the farmer's lost his mind in the storm. I'm in a two week hangover daze, barely on my feet, but I get closer, and I can finally make out what he's screamin' at me. 'Snakes! Snakes!' I look down and the whole cornfield is alive with snakes, all of them rialed outta their holes by that storm. I like to flew to that tractor."

"Jesus," Laney whispered in horror.

"Aw yeah. Just awful. Anyway, farmer took me back to his place. I spent the next three days cleanin' out his silos and then I hitched a ride to Fargo."

Laney turned and stared. "What happened to the woman? The barroom angel?"

Orley shrugged sadly. "I never went back. I think her name was Shirley. Shannon maybe. Shasta."

Laney squinted. "You- the truck?"

"Never saw it again. Just left it." It came out as a murmur.

"Well. There's something Gant doesn't know."

"I wonder what happened to her all the time," Orley confessed. "I can still picture her face clear as day."

Laney didn't know what to say so he got back to work. Behind him, Orley did too.

"What about you son? You mean to tell me that in this whole wide world, there ain't a single person who'd miss you if you were gone? I mean, really? You washed out that bad? I left mine at the edge of a cornfield, but at least I had it."

Laney looked up. On the wall in front of him was a calendar from 1998, still on June. "Times are changing for me. I first rolled into New Mexico, I was so- so free of connection I probably almost drove right into space, hit a big bump and I woulda. I was a perfect candidate for alien abduction when I got out here." Laney cleared his throat and opened the second to last drawer. "I drove into Roswell last month to look at the UFO museum. Beautiful town. Wide and flat like a pancake made outta Legos." He paused. "Stopped by this drive through for coffee. Big Donut. It's the one with the big brown donut on the roof. I'll be damned if the most beautiful woman I ever seen wasn't working the window. I mean, she's not scary beautiful, like she'd be mean or cruel or anything. Nah. She's natural pretty, the real kind that's in the eyes and the hands."

Orley cackled.

"Yeah whatever." Laney gave him a dark look. "I had a few days to kill before I had to be back out here and I was sleeping in my truck, so that night I got a room in the Motel 6 so I could take a shower and wash my shirts in the bathtub."

"I do that."

"So you know. Hit 'em with the hair dryer, done deal. And the Motel 6 shampoo is good for shaving, way better than the soap in the

Starbucks bathroom. Anyway, next morning I go back to Big Donut and I see her again. And I could tell, I swear, I could tell she was glad to see me."

"There ya go."

"Yeah, so I get a donut. Just glazed, nothing fancy, and she seemed to like that. Showing off donut lore, my extensive knowledge of the product, it wasn't the right time."

"Wise."

"I give her my best smile and she gives me one back. Whole rest of the day I was on a cloud. Went back the next day and did the same thing. Day four, I still can't work up the nerve to ask her out and I swear, on day four she asks me if I wanna eat dinner with her at the ten dollar all-you-can-eat steakhouse buffet."

"Skip to the good part, kid. What happened in the parking lot after the chow. And tell me about her caboose."

Laney scowled. "We ate and then we drove out to the old drive in and had wine coolers. They still make 'em, I mean I had no idea. Maria tells me about her brothers and her parents, shit like that. I just listened. She likes knitting. Uses real wool, too. Vegetable dyes. The next night I had dinner at her place. Little trailer, and that don't sound like much but she has it fixed up real nice."

"What'd ya have?"

"Chicken fried steak with white gravy and green beans. Mashed potatoes, too. And she made peach cobbler."

"Goddamn," Orley marveled in a faraway voice. "That right there would be my last meal."

"It was damn good. Anyway, now we text back and forth every night."

"She know you're a shit shoveling bum who works at The Rock Shack?"

"You mean does she know I'm a geology enthusiast with a solid gig just outside The Valley of Fires? Working in tourism? She does."

"I'll have to remember that," Orley said wryly. "Geology enthusiast." Laney gave him a sidelong glance.

"I even told her about you, Orley."

"Did you now." Orley pretended like he didn't care.

"Bowlegged old jackass, smells like onions and something you might find in a trash bag behind a crooked taxidermy outfit. Egg salad for jewelry, boots held together with horse glue and dried swamp algae, the-"

"Jackpot," Orley interrupted. He raised what looked like an old photograph and studied it carefully. Laney quickly crossed around and looked over his shoulder.

"A young Mr. Gant," Laney breathed.

The picture was of Gant, some thirty years younger. He was fit, with a military crew cut, standing next to another man who looked much the same. Both of them were smiling. The low ridge in the background was unmistakable. They were here, right where The Rock Shack stood.

"Look closer boy," Orley whispered.

"The other dude's belt buckle," Laney whispered back.

Laney backed away as the gears in his mind caught, then rushed out of the office to the cash register. It was dark, so Laney turned on the old lamp by the register to use as a spotlight. "Orley! Bring that out here!"

Orley drifted out and handed him the photo, perplexed. Laney raised the magnifying glass they kept in front for the customers to inspect the rocks and looked at the picture with it, holding it in the bright pool of lamplight, then stiffened and handed both items to Orley.

"I knew it." Laney said softly. "Check it out. Look at the other dude's left hand."

Orley peered through the magnifying glass. "What am I looking for? The guy has the same buckle all right, way small of course, but... Holy shit." Orley lowered the magnifying glass. The photo fell from his limp hand. The magnifying glass cracked when he dropped it, too. Orley sagged back into the counter, stunned.

"A wedding ring." Laney looked out the window. "If I'm right- if we're right- then... Somewhere out there is a giant fucking wedding ring."

Orley cackled, an insane sound, then stopped, stunned that it had come from him. Laney turned to him, alarmed. The old cowboy cackled again, an unhinged studder of laughter that seemed to erupt from him like a seizure. He looked at Laney with wide eyes.

"You realize what this means, don't you?"

Laney shook his head. Orley barked again and held his sides.

"We're dead, boy! It means we're dead!"

4

Laney took another long pull off the bottle and handed it back to Orley, who drank with refined abandon. There was something impressive about the casual way the old man handled the bottle, the full and throaty chug he put on it, and even his closing gasp of relish and his gassy afterthought belch had flair. They'd taken two folding patio chairs out onto the porch and started on the whiskey without a word. They were both certain, in a deep and stricken way, that there was a huge gold wedding ring out there in the sand, waiting to be uncovered in the morning. The night seemed colder than it really was. The starry sky was a hard, deep void, glowing with flecks of corruption, and the arid wind was filled with sorrow, like it was borrowed from the background of a movie about death, gun smoke, and cholera. Laney thought about Maria, trying to bring light to his mind, but he kept coming back to the aching conclusion that he'd never see her again. It was simply too dangerous. He'd come between a rich man and his gold, and there was no way to reverse out of the wreckage. Gant had his social security number and a copy of his Idaho driver's license. If he ran, Gant could and would hunt him down. If he tried to hand over the gold, Laney knew he'd never leave this patch of New Mexico. Even knowing about it would be too much in Gant's eyes. He'd probably be buried in the hole the buckle came out of. Orley was probably thinking the same thing while he drank and burped and sighed and stared with glassy eyes at their small future. They were walking the green mile and they both knew it.

"Shit," Orley said softly, mostly to himself. It was the first time he'd spoken in more than an hour.

"Yep."

"I wonder who the buckle guy was." Orley sipped again. The bottom of the bottle was close, but Orley didn't seem any drunker than usual. "How the fuck did belt buckle guy... how the fuck did he become a giant who got lost in time?"

"I bet he was a nice dude."

Orley squinted at him, mildly curious. "How you figure?"

"Mr. Gant is a dick. Drives a new Cadillac and looks down on my truck. Always has some kind of asshole judgment in his eyes. Even when he was trying to be nice during his recruitment, I knew he was a dick. That night at the bar when he was first telling me about this place and the job? He treated the waitress like shit. Total contempt. It was embarrassing, but what kind of guy does that? Nah. Mr. Gant isn't a good guy. Means the dead guy was. It's the, like, the mathematics of people. Good guys and bad guys and whatnot. You get it."

"I do." Orley shifted a little in his chair. "Pretty comic book, but it holds water. Adds up in more ways than one, you think on it. You know what kind of man is rude to waiters and waitresses?"

"Guy who likes pee and armpit in his food?"

"A fool."

"How is that useful, Orley? The guy has power. I mean he drives a new Cadillac kind of power. He has everything he needs to bring the hammer down on us and he will."

"Maybe." Orley'd been in a deep and boozy meditation and something had cooked inside him. He lit a cigarette and gestured with it. "I say we go find that ring, saw some off and run for it. You go left, I go right, and we run like bastards until Gant's hired killers catch up to us. Good month or two if we don't get popped before we make it out of New Mexico. We keep it aimless and we might make it." He took a drag and blew a slow plume. "Can't catch a man who don't have a map."

"There's gotta be a better way." Laney kept thinking about Maria. There had to be a road back to Big Donut. Back to that trailer, with the peach cobbler and all the rest. An unlikely life had begun to form in front of him, like a tomato seedling growing from a kitchen sponge. "I don't want to go the unmapped route, Orley. I wanna get back to my chick. I wanna keep being Laney Bozeman."

Orley roused himself. "What if- what if you called him and told him I found a glass eye. A great big glass eye. You know, buried out there in lot nine. And then I- I-"

Laney sat up straight. "And then you freaked out and joined a traveling Pentecostal church! Tents, snakes, tongues, the whole nine yards."

Orley snapped his fingers. "Bingo. He'll tell you he wants to come see the eye. Then we jump him. He won't know about the gold, he'll think we just found a big glass ball."

"Right." Laney smoothed back his hair. "This is good, Orley. If we tell him we found the ring he'll show up with hired muscle and then it's game over. But a glass eye? He'll come alone. When he gets here we convince him that we know what happened, even though we got no idea, and we'll turn him in if he doesn't make a deal. You know, guarantee our safety, maybe a finder's fee, shit like that. Then we part ways."

Orley stared, aghast. "Ain't no parting ways here dipshit. We kill 'em. We have to. That man is too dangerous to leave in our trail. Me an' you are digging out here because this ring is a secret worth killing for. We're halfway through a case of premeditated murder and we're the victims! Just a matter of time, but we been set up to take the long fall."

"No," Laney said firmly. "No way. I'm not killing anybody, and neither are you. He'll kill us for sure if he gets a chance, I can feel it too, but we have to be better than that, Orley." Laney looked at him. "I mean, I'm better than that. Maybe you are too. Or you could be."

Orley spat but said nothing. Laney realized they were both just killing time. Neither of them wanted to go out into the desert to hunt for a supernaturally huge object by flashlight, especially one with their doom wrapped around it.

"We just need dirt on the guy. He has to have done something illegal. I mean think about it." Laney sat back and rubbed his chin. "Gold, seems like most of it has blood on it. This gold here is certainly no exception."

Laney rose and paced. He was past buzzed and quickly approaching drunk. "We need more. There wasn't shit in those file cabinets. Nothing else in the desk. There's nothing in this house. We don't have any way to research anything. We can't call anybody because we don't know anybody we can trust."

"You got the donut girl."

"No way I'm bringing her into this." Laney looked up at the night sky. "No. We got shit, Orley. We need to find a way to get the truth out of Gant. That's what we need. The truth will set us free. Just like it says in the bumper stickers."

"We could torture him," Orley mused. "Knives. Ants." He looked at the tip of his burning cigarette.

"No." Laney sat back down and rubbed his face. "What do we know about Gant? Other than the food contamination moron thing?"

"Told me once he thought Sandra Bullock had a nice rear end."

"He drives that new Cadillac. Always a year or two old."

"Roundish, he said. But then he also enjoys the Tom Cruise movies. The spy ones." Orley shook his head to clear it. "You even know where he lives?"

Laney wracked his memory. "Reno, I think. Or maybe Santa Fe. Might have houses in both places. Nowhere close enough to stop by and mess with us on a regular basis. He's the type who would pop in for surprise inspections if he was right next door."

"Rolex watch. New car. Bitches about his swimming pool. He's got that rich man glow too, like he moisturizes or takes the forehead Botox like a magazine lady."

"Always wears a brand new tracksuit."

Orley snorted. "And them running shoes."

"Never laughs."

"When he does he sounds like an actor. I heard it once. Made my skin crawl."

"Hmm. No accent."

Orley drank and went quiet. Maybe he was thinking about the lightning woman in North Dakota, or maybe he was thinking nothing at all. Laney closed his eyes. Right now, Maria was probably closing up for the day, getting ready to go home. She'd check the restrooms, do the till, maybe box up a couple stray glazed for a neighbor because she was kind that way. And then she'd go home, to her little trailer in the little trailer park, and watch TV. Laney wished he was sitting on the couch next to her, drinking a cup of coffee after a long day at some shit job. They'd eat beans and rice with a couple tortillas because they were poor and they lived in a trailer, but they'd be the kind of happy that a man like Gant could never afford and probably didn't even know about. Daydreaming was Laney's primary vehicle for understanding his life, and it told him that he wasn't where he belonged. It also put a dark face on the doings at The Rock Shack. Strange, bad things, giant things were happening here.

"Orley," Laney said slowly, "you ever wonder if you're in the wrong place at the wrong time? Like over and over again?" Orley roused himself and glared at him.

"You mean do I wonder if I'd be better off without you right now? Yep. Anything like that you can answer for yourself, Bozeman."

"Ha ha." Laney shook his head. "No, I mean, I was thinking just now about how the life I want for myself, my vision of my best possible future- there isn't any gold in it."

"Commie."

"Gant thought it was worth running this place for years. The man is gold crazy, clear as day now. You can't tell me he's a happy man, either. And so far, all this gold has done for us is drive you crazy and I had to sleep outside. And it don't look like it's gonna get better anytime soon."

"All true," Orley admitted, surprising Laney. "I'm sittin' here wondering something way bigger, son. Maybe it's that giant buckle in there, putting shit in perspective for us, but I'm thinkin' I never been to France. Never been to one of them little French nightclubs with the fruity trombone music, all fulla smoke and armpits and thick red wine. I never punched a movie star. I never snorkeled in Bimini, and I never drank champagne out of a high heel shoe. Never wrecked a Limousine. Shit. We die out here in the middle of nowhere we both failed big time, and failure is a shit thing go large on."

Laney got up and went back inside, into the kitchen. The beans were almost done. He took the dried California chilis out and stemmed and seeded a dozen, then put them in a second pot with two cups of water, a little salt, four garlic cloves and a splash of oil. He'd seen a man make red sauce on late night TV once, and this is how he did it, even though he suspected Maria would disapprove. He brought the pot to a boil and then covered it and let it sit and steam. While that was going on, he took six of the now frozen tamales out of the freezer and peeled the skins off, then set them in a pan. When the chilis were soft, he dumped the whole thing, water and all, into the ancient Jetson's blender he'd picked up at a flea market for a dollar and blended it into a sauce. Humming now, Laney dumped half of the sauce off into an old pickle jar and the rest into the pinto beans.

Orley drifted in and crashed down at the kitchen table without a word. Laney cranked the burner under the tamales and fried them, and when the masa was browned and crunchy, he splashed them with red sauce and fried that a little, too. They ate beans and tamales in silence. Orley snorted and made satisfied animal grunts, but he made no conversation and Laney was glad for that. It was a strange thing, knowing there might be a fortune out there waiting to be discovered in the morning, and neither man was happy about it. The unhappiness was confusing and wrong, and the only good thing about the night was dinner.

5

Orley took the bedroom again and fell into a deep, gurgling sleep almost instantly, leaving Laney alone. He drifted back out onto the porch and sat down. They would look for the ring in the morning light, and if they found it, they found it. If they didn't, they'd have to accept that they ransacked The Rock Shack and lost their jobs because they were idiots who'd been driven mad by a giant belt buckle, and that the buckle itself was nothing more than an old Sears display or part of a Bob's Big Boy statue someone threw off a passing truck years ago. He thought about that until he was tired enough to go back in and lay on the couch.

Instead of sleeping, Laney studied the belt buckle. This was deep water. His first problem was sleeping in the next room. Mr. Gant would certainly hunt him to the ends of the Earth if there really was a ring out there, but Ralston Orley might kill him instantly as soon as they found it. Laney was only useful until that moment. After that, he was in the crosshairs of everyone. Orley had already tossed around murder and torture as workable ideas, and he'd done it in a casual way, too. And Orley had a gun. Laney had a hunting knife he used for cheese, and it was under the seat in his truck.

He wasn't thinking clearly, he realized, and it wasn't the whiskey. His buzz had worn off while he was making the tamales. Laney didn't care for drinking on the same level as Orley, and that was good, he reasoned, because even sober he made bad decisions. With a clear head, he'd taken a job at The Rock Shack, working for a man who wouldn't care if he died in a wild boar attack as long as he didn't have to work the next day. He worked with a drunk he feared might kill him in his sleep over an imaginary giant ring. He needed to use his head, and it was dawning on him that this was a new development.

In spite of himself, Laney smiled. If he had a rubber snake, this would be the time to use it. He imagined sneaking into the bedroom and laying it on Orley's chest, then stepping outside and banging on a piece of roofing tin to simulate thunder, like they'd done in old radio shows. What would Orley do? Wet himself? Scream out the lightning bar angel's name so they might finally know it? Shoot himself in the foot?

Laney's smile faded. He shouldn't even be in the bungalow. It was just possible that Orley was actually awake, faking the moist sleep apnea and waiting for Laney to drift off. Slowly, quietly, Laney rose and slipped out the front door. He'd sleep in the back of his truck again. If Orley planned to kill him, he'd have to crunch across the gravel first. It was something.

Once he was under his old blanket, situated and warm, Laney took out his phone and checked to see if Maria sent him a message. The reception was terrible and flickered between one bar and nothing, but there was one new text. It had come in late last night, a smiley face emoji. Laney sent one back, even though he knew it might take a day or two to make it. Then he looked at the stars. He'd entered a world of murder, giants, and intrigue. There was a chance he would prevail. There was also a chance he would be fired and possibly sued in small claims court. There was a chance he would die a lonesome and pitiful death and be buried in the hole a giant belt buckle had come from. Really, anything could happen.

Giant things could happen.

The thought woke him. Even Ralston Orley knew it, with his talk of French snorkels and whatnot. Laney took his phone out and checked the time. It wasn't especially late, but he had no bars. There was one place where his cellphone worked reliably. Martin's, the lonely gas station twenty miles East. It would be good to show his face at the station, too, and leave a trail of potential clues in case he wound up in the buckle hole after all.

Moving quickly and quietly, Laney rolled up his blankets and tossed them in the cab, then gently opened the gate. He turned the headlights on when he was a hundred yards away. Martin's Gasoline was still open when he got there, but Laney stopped short and cut the lights and the engine. Wanda Kemper was in there and the lights were on, but she was probably sleeping. Martin's was old, dating from the early sixties, and there had been several owners. Laney heard the entire history of the gas station one night at a bar in Socorro. The founder was Martin Gredvig, a hobby astronomer who moved to New Mexico from Chicago and started the gas station and garage with his wife. They sold it when they retired to the Chavez family, who ran it for twenty years and were known far and wide as trustworthy and capable mechanics. They sold the place and moved to Las Cruces, and then came a string of shady New Yorkers, then a few shady people from Albuquerque, and then finally a retired schoolteacher named Wanda Kemper. The hard old woman made out like a bandit on bottled water, but she also had soda and junk food. Laney checked his phone. Two bars. His heart rate jumped as he hit the button for Maria.

"Laney?" She sounded surprised and a little sleepy.

"Maria! I had to run an errand so I'm- I have reception. For the moment."

"Oh good! How's it going out there?"

Laney swallowed. "Fine. Just fine." There was an awkward pause.

"So what's up?" He could almost hear her smile, even though such a thing was impossible. "You just call to hear my voice?"

"Pretty much."

"Romantic." Maria sounded pleased. Laney closed his eyes. "I was just thinking about you, Laney."

"I was thinking about you too." Laney opened his eyes. Martin's looked like something out of a movie in that instant, the bleached old sign a yellow beacon. "The old guy stuck around this time. Ralston Orley."

"The man you don't get along with? I hope it's working out."

"Yeah, it's cool I guess. We got to talking and you know, he's deeper than I thought he was. Sometimes, anyway. He thinks big thoughts when he has to."

"Like what?"

"Like France." Laney smiled. "Can you imagine a day when we go to France? Me an' you? We could check out a jazz band in a little club and drink fancy wine and eat cheese."

There was an overlong pause. "Have you been drinking? You sound different."

"Just a little. And that was before dinner." Laney sighed. "I'm fine."

"France." Maria sipped something, and ice tinkled in the glass. "I guess I can see that, but if we were gonna go somewhere on the other side of the whole world, I don't know why we wouldn't go to Spain. I speak the language and they have all kinds of special ham and man, they even got these little red oranges. I saw it in a magazine. Why, ah, what got you all the way to thinking about France?"

"The stars." Laney leaned back and looked up, out the side window. "The world, life, everything is bigger than I thought it was."

Maria laughed, but she didn't say anything. She already knew the size of reality, he guessed.

"Things are weird out here," he continued lamely.

"Sounds like it. You get some good stuff at the store? I know you were worried."

"Tamales," Laney said with satisfaction. "Roasted pork and green chili. I got some dried red chilis to make sauce. Beans, too."

"How'd you learn to make red sauce? Your mamma didn't teach you. Not in Idaho."

She was fishing for details about his family again. This time Laney gave in. It didn't seem to matter as much anymore. He was usually too embarrassed to talk about it, but the grand scheme of things had changed.

"I learned pancakes from my grandma. She raised me, her and my grandpa. Lennette and Arnie. No aunts, no uncles, no brothers or sisters. Just me and them. Arnie passed, oh, must have been ten years ago now. When Gramma Lennette died the bank took the house and I got the truck. But I learned enough from those two about learning, so I guess that's where I picked up the how to on red sauce."

"I got a big enough family for both of us," Maria gushed, satisfied. "They're gonna love you, Laney. Now, my brothers, they might not be so warm at first and they're sorta- eh, they can be scary, especially Miguel, but they're all just sweet as can be when you get to know them. My mother, she isn't going to like you right away either, she's always so suspicious, she gets it from her shows, you'll see. And my father! Oh boy! You just let me handle Papa. Probably don't talk to him or make eye contact at first. You ever had a neighbor with a bad dog? It's like that, but-"

"What would you do if, oh, I dunno, if you could do anything?" Laney asked, changing the subject. "Like if money wasn't an issue. If you were rich."

"Get health insurance." Maria thought a little more. "I guess I might buy the donut shop from Mr. Murphy. Or start my own. Maybe... Maybe I'd go to France with you and eat cheese." She laughed again, that throaty, musical laugh. "I'd probably just have babies and get old just like everybody else." He could hear the smile in her voice. "That's for sure what I'd do."

Laney smiled, too. "That's pretty big."

After they hung up, Laney sat there looking at the stars. He was thinking about the distance between them all, reportedly huge beyond rational comprehension, when movement caught his eye. Wanda Kemper wobbled out of the gas station and lit a cigarette, puffed gently and stared at the road. Wanda was in her fifties or maybe her seventies, it was hard to tell. The blazing sun, dry winds, and bitter nights had scoured and smoothed the time in her in some way. Lean, tough, always in jeans and flannel, and her hair was short and grayish blond and she clearly cut it herself. Laney watched as she looked up at the Martin's Gasoline sign and for a moment it seemed like she was talking to it. The desert sank into everyone's mind eventually. Finally, she ground the cigarette out and went back inside. The station lights stayed on. Laney started the engine. It was time to say hello and maybe fish for some information.

The TV was on when he entered. The gas station was small, with two rows of junk ranging from spark plugs and dusty plastic jugs of anti-freeze to chips and candy, plus a cooler of overpriced bottled water and a small soda machine. Wanda was sitting in the register cockpit with her heels on the counter, arms behind her head. She glanced at Laney and returned her attention to the tiny television. Laney walked over to the soda machine, pulled a big paper cup from the slot, dumped in some ice and filled it with root beer. Then he drifted over to the counter and looked at the television, too. Wanda was watching the national news.

"Blood and guts," she reported without looking away. "If it ain't too terrible to know about then they don't want us knowin' it." She glanced over. Her eyes were big and the same blue as old denim. "Just the soda?"

"Yep." Laney fished his wallet out and put a five on the counter. Wanda stood and glanced at the TV again, then gave Laney a crooked smile.

"You road crew?"

"Work over at The Rock Shack. I drove on over to get cell reception so I could call my girl."

"You work with Ralson Orley!" Wanda cackled. "I thought you looked familiar. You came in one time lookin' for somethin', I forget."

"Edible food."

"Right!" Wanda cocked her head and gave him an almost sympathetic look. "Special is such a strange word anymore, ain't it?"

Laney looked back at the two aisles. Wanda sold expired pretzels and stale chips that were supremely unhealthy even when they were factory new, and she even had a few jars of a bright yellow cheese sauce that was probably made from recycled Halloween masks. Laney turned back to Wanda and shrugged.

"You know Orley then."

"Oh yeah." Wanda chuckled. "Old boy comes around now and again. You two get on?"

Laney shrugged again. "We got a temporary truce. He ain't that bad."

"Ain't what ya call good neither." Wanda shook her head. "We had us some fun though. Ole Ralston drove on up last Christmas Eve, I guess he was out at The Shack workin'. Me and him and Burt Garver from the weight station got into a potted ham right here at the counter. Just the three of us, diggin' it out with plastic forks, little Bing Crosby on the radio. Best damn Christmas dinner ever." She winked. "Rounded it out with the old mustard packets I still got from the hot dog days."

Last Christmas, Laney almost ate dinner at the Hungarian restaurant in Ruidoso, surrounded by glamorous California ski bums. After he looked at the menu, he drank one beer and watched other people eat instead. Later that night he ate a microwave bean burrito outside 7-11. It snowed that night, and he'd watched as it slowly turned the truck windows white. In the morning he could barely feel his feet, even though he'd slept with his boots on. At the time it seemed like an adventure, but now, looking back, it was different, like he was seeing the memory with someone else's eyes. Laney shook it off.

"You know Gant? Guy who owns the place?"

Wanda made a face. "He ain't one for chit chat. Old Freddy Tamayo, when he worked out at your rock stand, he used to come around from time to time and get a soda and shoot the shit." She shrugged. "Some people like a little company, you know? Your Mr. Gant ain't one of 'em."

"Freddy say anything else about him?"

"Well now..." Wanda squinted, looking back. The lines around her eyes were deep and defined, and her skin was more wooden than leathery. "Freddy thought the man might have been down on Mexicans but after a while, he realized he was just down on the workin' man. You know the type. Ain't a fat cat you gotta be some kinda loser." Wanda's eyes narrowed. "Secretive too. Ole Freddy thought he mighta been one of them rich folk collects antique doll heads or foreign toilet seats. Why so curious?" She grinned at him then. "Lemme guess. The diggin'. He got you boys diggin' like prairie dogs, am I right?"

Laney sucked on his straw and shrugged with his eyes. "Some."

"Had Freddy on the shovel too. Real hardass about it. You know what he got you boys lookin' for out there?"

"Rocks." It came out flat and bored as Laney could make it.

"Gold." Wanda took a breath through her nose. "The fool. Conquistadors came through here after it. They wanted to strike it rich like Cortés did down south. Juan de Oñate, now there's a story for ya. Juan went big. Son of a silver mogul outta Zacatecas, he thought fortune was his birthright. Him and his posse of dipshits came in hard and lost it all. Natives hated his ass, his boys figured him for incompetent, after he crapped out everyone wrote him off as another finger sniffin' mamma's boy." Wanda smiled proudly. "Oh yeah. This is The Land of Disappointment for a man chasin' the numbers."

Laney nodded. Wanda gestured at him with her chin.

"How 'bout you fella? You don't come off as a hustler. What brought you to these parts? I mean why in the world are you workin' at a place like The Rock Shack instead of..." Wanda shrugged and eyed him.

"No idea," Laney replied honestly. "I mean... I guess I was driving, maybe I was headed to Texas, can't even remember. Stopped in Ruidoso and I saw a sign for day work. One day led to another and then, shit, here I am."

"Pretty much describes how the cavemen rolled," Wanda marveled. "They just kinda went with it. The original drifters." She considered. "I guess that's how I wound up here too, now I think on it."

Laney nodded and waited for more.

"I was a schoolteacher. Topeka, Kansas. Met an ole boy with a stick on him name a Clancy and I'll be damned if we didn't decide to pack it in and head for sunny California, land of the avocado toast."

"And you stopped here?"

"Yep. Clancy ditched me right here at this very station. Martin's Gasoline. It was for sale and I had a couple bucks, I got my pension, shit. Happy an' content don't have as much in common as you think. That's what I learned right then anyway." She nodded, almost talking to herself now. "You can find all kinds of things out here, but most of 'em are things you weren't even looking for."

Laney digested that for a moment, then, quietly- "You find, like, happy or content... I don't get it."

Wanda looked out the window. Laney did, too. She was quiet for so long that it became awkward, and he was about to just leave like nothing happened when she spoke in the singsong storyteller cadence she might have used while addressing the Martin's Gasoline sign.

"I've beheld... shit." Wanda stepped closer to the window and looked up. "From my vantage point, here on the outskirts of civilization, I've seen wonderous lights in the sky. I felt strange vibrations in the earth that sang like a choir through the arroyos. Once I swear it rained tiny black seeds that turned to crows." Her voice lowered to a breath. "I seen secrets eaten whole and dreams writ backward, the rise and ruin of men and women alike, and I heard... I heard..."

Laney leaned in to catch the last of it.

"Inside the shadow of everything, curled like smoke below all the gossip and rumor and confusion is... well. There's often a strange truth that's hard to behold." She snapped out of it with a start and gave Laney a final wink.

"Give Ralston a pinch on the fanny for me, hear?"

6

"Wake up dummy."

Laney woke with a start. Orley was beside the truck, looming over him with a black expression. Adrenaline blazed through Laney in a painful electric explosion, and he hurled his blankets aside and sprang at the startled man in one fluid motion. Orley chirped and skipped back, and Laney fell into the gravel face first, scrambled quickly to his feet and held out his fists, crouched and snarling. Then he straightened. Orley was holding a cup of coffee in each hand, staring at him like he was an animal.

"What the hell is wrong with you boy!" Orley held out one of the cups, scowling. "I made coffee." Then his face split into a knowing, evil leer. "You thought I was gonna kill you just now, didn't you?" He snorted and spit. "Dipshit. We ain't even found the ring yet."

Laney took the coffee and sucked in a deep breath. He was shaking. The sky was just turning blue on the eastern horizon, and the first desert bird called out, soft and low. It was the last moment before the blazing dawn, right before the quiet blue world filled with golden yellow and long black shadows.

"You scared the hell out of me, Orley." Laney took another deep breath and blew it out slowly. A cool breeze stirred his hair and chilled the sweat that had bloomed on his forehead. "Man. Man. Almost gave me a heart attack. Your morning face is terrifying."

"Early bird gets the worm." Orley chuckled and slapped his gut. "My bladder is the finest alarm clock in the nation. Ain't gonna beat Ralston

Orley off the line, no sir. Half hour before sunrise and I'm lookin' for a commode."

"Good for you." The coffee was absolutely terrible, dark and bitter and burnt. It dawned on Laney then that Orley hadn't made coffee at all, he'd just refried the pot from yesterday until it turned into a flavored acid.

"Made breakfast, too." Orley said it with great pride and stolid reserve, like he'd performed a miracle but didn't want any praise. "While you getting you beauty sleep, I mean."

Laney pulled his boots on and followed Orley back inside, tossing his coffee as he walked. The buckle was right where they left it, no bigger and no smaller. Orley walked past it without a glance and sat down at the kitchen table. There were two bowls, one full and one empty. Cold beans, straight from the can.

"I'll make new coffee."

"Hoped you would." Orley lit a cigarette. "I was thinking about that glass eye bit. We were on to something there."

"In the bright, nervous hell of morning it sounds just insane enough to work." Laney put the filter in the old machine and dumped in a double heaping of grounds. "He'll panic. That's what we need to drill into. We need Gant to lose his shit in a big way. Then we're on even ground."

"If we can trip him up enough to get the goods on him, we can make it out," Orley agreed. "He panics half as much as you did just now, shit, the old boy might even have a stroke. Done deal."

"One of us has to call him." Laney sat down. "But first, we go out and look for the ring. If we find it, I'll call Gant and tell him you found, shit, I'll tell him you found the buckle and dragged it into the living room. And then you lost your mind. It has the merit of being true."

Orley glowered and smoked, slowly nodding.

"I tell him you lit out with religion," Laney continued. "Headed back to Pensacola to reunite with your spiritual kin. He'll come alone because he'll think I'm here all by myself and I don't know anything about a ring. When he does, we grill him. You got a gun, I got a clear head."

Orley nodded. "We remove me from his picture so I can pull off a sneak attack, and we get him out here in an easy way that makes it seem like he don't need to bring muscle." Orley puffed thoughtfully. "I like it."

"We'll hide your truck in the ravine across the road."

"Okay. Let's work this through. Gant pulls up, he comes in and you hit him with the news? Then I come in hard?"

"Yes, yes," Laney said shortly. "I mean no. You give me a few minutes to talk to him. I tell him we know what's really going on here. Then he lies and *then* you come in hard. So wait about five minutes. And no shooting, no torture, nothing like that. I just see what he says. He'll spin a web of bullshit, but we might be able to read between the lines. Who knows? Maybe he'll just fess up. He might even ask for help."

"I got no idea how a man turns into a giant and walks back through time, but we find that ring? Means Gant knew it was out there all along and he knows exactly what happened. And there has to be something illegal about that, Laney, and I mean the bad kind of illegal. I don't know what and neither do you, so he has to talk, and I mean spill wide open. Or he has to try to kill you. That'll do, too. We need conviction dirt we can blackmail him with and we got one shot."

Laney got up and poured two cups of coffee. "Me and him talking is a good start. Me and him talking with you pointing a gun at him is a strong finish."

Orley sipped and nodded his appreciation. The sun gradually rose. Laney made them a breakfast of scrambled eggs with broken tamales, and they ate in silence. When they were done, they got shovels on the side of the bungalow and walked out into the desert.

7

⚬❈⚬

"Here's where I found the buckle."

They stood at the edge of lot nine, about a quarter mile from The Rock Shack. A lizard watched them from the shade of a stunted piñon pine on the far side of the hole. The air smelled of creosote, desert sage, and fine rock dust. The bright blue sky was clear of clouds, and a lone contrail cut a sharp line through the southeast. Laney looked at the hole. Orley looked at Laney, watching him think.

"Okay," Laney said eventually. "The buckle was just under the surface, kinda poking out in some places, right?"

Orley nodded. "Wind must have uncovered it for the day. Next wind woulda dusted it over again. Pure luck I found it."

"All right then." Laney turned and looked back in the direction of The Rock Shack. "Now if that buckle was on the belt of a giant, he was facing that way when he fell. Toward the road. And he fell on his back."

Orley looked back. "Yeah. I guess."

"Question is when he fell, did he flail, or did he just fall like a board? I'm guessing arms out. People fall, their arms go out to the sides. Least I think they do."

Orley squinted at the hole. "Big man. Buckle that size, I reckon we're lookin' at maybe a hundred feet tall. More."

"Let's walk it off." Laney turned and pointed. "Fifty paces that way, then thirty that way. Be about where a hand would be, give or take."

They started walking, scanning the ground.

"You trust me Laney?" Orley asked out of the blue.

"Hell no."

"I don't trust you either. Fact is I thought you might kill me in my sleep."

Laney laughed without humor. "That's why I slept outside. I even thought there might be poison in those cold beans."

Orley was silent for a few paces. "Gant is counting on us never getting along. It's insurance in case we figured it out. I was thinkin' on it all night while I was waiting for you to sneak in and slit my throat. We both shovel, we got that in common. No people to look for us, we got that too, but the last part of Gant's perfect triangle is who we are, Laney. We ain't the type to come out on top. S'why we're here. Gant planned this out like a master. He hired losers to lose."

They reached fifty paces, or there about. Laney turned and began marching. Orley walked beside him, studying the sand.

"I guess it's time for us to, like, bloom or whatever," Laney said, distracted. "What are you gonna do with your cut of the gold?"

"I ain't even thought about it." Orley sounded bitter.

"Don't lie to me. Tell me man. Dreams are what sets us apart from, I dunno. Mildew. You got a dream, that means you got an endgame. A throughline. Losers don't have that."

"You first."

"Fine. I get a chunk of gold I'm starting a grocery store. Don't laugh. We live in a food desert man. The nearest good grocery store is in Albuquerque and that town is too dangerous to blow through just for apples and spinach. Good food rolls through on its way east and west. I worked in this little place in Santa Fe? Shit man, they had fresh fruit all year round, always had greens, bulk organic hippy stuff galore, and they even had this canned soup from India that tasted like flowers. And don't get me started on the beer."

"Starter up, by all means."

"There is good beer everywhere, Orley. Literally every state makes some kind of pilsner or lager. You got your wheat beers, your IPAs, all the golden ales and bitter ales. But within a hundred miles of where we stand? American factory light. Shit probably has termites in it. I think it's all actually made out of expired Dollar General rice and mutant corn, like the z-list crap they can't even use for pig food."

They stopped walking. Right there, just poking through the surface of the hardpack sand and rock, was an expanse of gold the size of a dinner platter. Neither man moved. Laney felt his life change then, as if someone had turned a page in the book of his existence. His mouth went dry and he glanced at Orley, who was staring at the gold with an expression that looked painful on his pockmarked face. Wonder mixed with relief, peppered with delight, and flushed with triumph, but all of it mixed with a boyishness that had not visited Orley's face since his first bad day as a bad young man.

"I'm gonna spend mine on women." Orley looked up and grinned like an old wolf standing over a pot roast. "Wild women and booze."

8

"Ah, Mr. Gant? It's Laney Bozeman out at The Rock Shack."

"What is it, Bozeman." There was a rustle, like Gant was roosting in a nest of newspapers. "What the hell time is it?"

"Nine PM sir. Sorry to call so late but I have a situation here."

Laney and Orley had spent the entire day digging the gold ring out of the rocky ground, laboring hard, and when they were finally done they stared at it until just before sunset. It was more than twice the size of a manhole cover and thicker than a car tire. Unlike the buckle, which had been flat on the ground and just below the surface, the ring was buried sideways, so the final hole exposing it was five feet deep and six feet wide. Something that might have been bone ran through the center where the finger might have been, but it crumbled to the touch, as light and powdery as dried sea foam. They estimated that the ring weighed between seven and nine hundred pounds, and they were rock men by trade, so their guesses were better than average. Gold came in at around twenty thousand a pound, so the ring in the hole before them was worth upward of fourteen million dollars. They walked back to the bungalow in a daze after that, and Orley went straight to the kitchen and hit the bottle. Laney joined him, but he didn't hit it quite as hard. It was shocking, what it had all come to. They ate dinner in silence as night fell. After that, they sat on the porch and argued over the details, and half a bottle later they psyched themselves up to make the call.

"What kind of situation." It wasn't a question. "If you're calling about the toilet again forget it. Fix it yourself or quit."

"Ah, no sir. It's Ralston Orley. I got here last night and he was still here, sitting on the couch and drunk as a skunk. In his underwear, sir, and I'm sorry to say I even saw one of his bare feet. He found a giant belt buckle in the sand out in lot nine and dragged it into the living room. Really screwed up the floor too. Sir." Laney swallowed. Beside him, Orley grinned and stifled a guffaw. Laney angled the old landline phone out so Orley could hear better.

"I see." Deadly serious. "Where is he now?"

"Gone sir. He left as soon as he was sober enough to drive. He was jabbering about the lord and serpents and he made no sense at all. The buckle is scary to look on, sir, and that's gotta be what broke him, the poor soul. I wanted to call this morning, but I had to clean the bathroom and then-"

"Stop! Stop talking, Bozeman. Did he find anything else out there?"

"No sir, just the buckle. Is there- there ain't another buckle out there, is there? This thing is spooky, I can't make that clear enough, sir. Drove Orley crazy like I said. I suppose I can go look but if-"

"Bozeman." Gant took a breath. "Laney. Take a break. Here's what I want you to do. Watch some TV. Can you do that?"

"TV. Yessir."

"You tell anybody about Orley or the buckle?"

"Nobody to tell, sir. So just you. Should I call someone?"

"Don't call anyone, you hear me?" Gant took a hissing breath, clearly out of patience. He tried for sweet then, and it came out like a teaspoon of warm, sugary snake venom. "Just sit tight. I'm in Reno. I'll be there at first light tomorrow, maybe a little later if there's traffic on my way out. You just sit tight. You did the right thing, calling me like this."

"Thank you, sir. I have to ask. This buckle- is it yours? I mean did you bury a giant belt buckle out here? It's really old, looks like, and I mean *old* old." Laney tried to sound lost and confused and he didn't have to stretch for it.

"Everything out there is mine," Gant said gravely. "I own that patch of New Mexico." Then it was back to poison sweet. "You just watch TV.

You want me to bring anything?" He sounded like a fast food manager offering a hairnet. "Beer? Ice cream?"

"I don't drink on duty, sir. And I'm lactose intolerant. But thank you."

Gant hung up. Laney and Orley burst out laughing.

"I don't drink," Orley howled. "Sir! An' I got the lactose fanny!" He saluted and almost fell out of his chair.

"That was good." Laney couldn't help but smile. Morning was a long night away. It gave them time to plot.

"Jesus Truck Repair in Ruidoso," Orley said when he caught his breath. "Rudy and them loco boys Frankensteined up a plasma torch that'll cut that ring. I'll straight up trade 'em Gant's Cadillac for it, that and one of their old tow trucks. We cut the ring and I'll use the tow winch to lever the sections into our truck beds, then you go left and I go right." He sighed. "This time tomorrow and I'll be halfway to the fabled land of undisclosed location."

"So we're definitely taking the gold." Laney cleared his throat. "Like, all of it."

Orley glared. "That man will kill us, Laney. He planned it out. You can't be this dumb. I mean you really can't. You'll get me killed."

"You thought it all through." Laney's sarcasm was lost on Orley, who nodded absently.

"I play dumb to confuse people."

Orley drank. They were halfway through Laney's second bottle of whiskey. Laney's mind had been whirling right up until the call and now it was blank and flat. His ears weren't ringing. His entire inner landscape was free of motion. He considered the problems before him, and nothing came to mind. Laney often suspected, especially when he was pondering his willful ignorance, that thinking was actually the act of listening closely to the workings of the mind, so he listened for a whisper of direction. All that came to him was the gurgle of Orley's intestines.

"Well, shit," he pronounced finally.

Orley gestured at him with the bottle. "Look up, son. You're either about to be rich or you're about to die. The wait is almost over. One way or another that big thing you always wondered about is finally here."

Laney snatched the bottle. "You really gonna spend your cut on crazy women and booze?"

"I am," Orley declared proudly. "I'm an ugly man, son. Maybe tomorrow I'll be a rich ugly man, but I'll always be ugly. I got terrible ways, too. Nah. I'd as soon pay a woman to deal with me and crazy lets you pay by the day. She'd deserve every last thousand dollar bill, too. World is full of bad men when you get right down to it and most of them bad men are cheap as hell, which makes 'em even worse. I won't put that sin on my scorecard. I know what I am, and I know what I'd charge to deal with me. That's what I'm willing to pay."

Laney didn't know what to say. He was as far from a therapist or a self-help guru as he'd ever been at that moment. It did strike him as European, bringing to mind a magazine he'd seen with a picture of sunbrowned fat men with gold jewelry aboard a shining white party yacht with the bikini models they were dating. It didn't seem worth mentioning, and those men might well have been from Texas or New Jersey.

"Far as the booze goes," Orley continued, "shit, no story there." Orley took the bottle back. "Once, I swear I caught the blues like it was a sickness. That was right around the time I met the Lightning Woman. I knew she was what I deserved, too, a woman who would ride me like a parade float until my heart tore apart and I dropped dead in my tracks, and then on she'd go, wherever the party took her. I mighta loved her, see, but she loved the edge of a kind of surging wave that travels through shit bars and taquerias and truck stops, those perfect windows where time stands still, when the magic touches them and sweeps on through, and for a little while I was riding along next to her." Orley took a deep breath and let it out slow. "Then that wave was done with me. You see the commercials on the TV, people are down everywhere so I ain't special. A lot of them are too poor to afford them pills, but ain't one of 'em too poor to hit a bottle, shit is practically free. That's a hard road and there ain't too many off ramps. I'll stay in my lane if you know what I mean."

"Oh yeah. Bum would squeeze out behind the dumpster, and I'd use a piece of cardboard as a scooper and get it up under the handle. First couple of times, boy, I'd never seen a man blow his stack like that. I'm talkin' bible fury. That first morning, he came out all high on his horse and opened his car door and stopped, raised his hand and sniffed it, got a little Hershey's kiss on the tip of his nose." Orley sighed in great satisfaction. "Howled. I mean he howled like a werewolf that just got the snip. Got worse as time wore on."

"Tell me." Laney sat back.

"The fool paid me to keep an eye on his car after the second time. Fifty cents a night. I'd hit it at my leisure and tell him I checked it. Jennings got to thinking that someone was watching him and that they knew to the minute when he'd leave. I left off after a while, just long enough for him to think it was over. Then I'd start again. Terrorized him for a year pretty solid, then it was on and off after I hit the road. I'd come back for Christmas sometimes, then again for Billy's birthday and to help out from time to time. I ever saw his car around Little Rock, I'd hit it again."

"Cold bro. Icy."

"Yep. Been workin' for peanuts ever since. Maybe it's true that you can't keep a good man down, but you can take an average man and grind on him until he's bad to the bone. Ain't nobody gonna argue with that."

"You should write lyrics for country songs, Orley. I can practically hear 'em now. Lightning Woman of Bismarck. Hobo Bamboozle. Rodeo Corndog Man."

Orley chuckled. "Goddamn Merl Haggard right there."

"My first job was bailing hay. Kittleman Ranch. I did other shit for 'em, too. Wired fences back together, washed the cars and trucks, dragged house trash down the main drive to the road. The owner was named Winston P. Harney. Huge mustache, an' I mean so burly it looked fake. Gentleman rancher, they call fellas like him. That's a rich guy from New York who lords over idiots like me and makes 'em do his ranching. His big job is posing for the pictures, all steely eyed and cool like he's the god of donkeys. I don't think I ever saw that man pick up a pinecone, much less a hammer or a shovel. He liked to hand out the pay personally, and he always gave everyone a long, searching look, real piercing, like he knew what you were really up to."

Orley spit again. He might not have been listening. It occurred to Laney then that Orley said he had no family.

"What happened to your brother?"

"Billy? First Gulf War."

"Shit. Sorry man." Laney leaned back.

"One time... One time, I don't know where the hell I was. Maybe the vet, maybe getting a tooth looked on, but I read a lobby magazine and there was an article about fly fishing in Patagonia."

"South America. Way down at the end."

Orley nodded. "That's right." He stared out into the darkness. "I always thought that if I got crazy enough, if I got that far out on the wires, if I was so down on my luck that it all ran cold, shit, I'd head to Patagonia. Toss my thumb out and ride to the border. Hop a train after that. Then I'd hit the jungle and fight my way through, and then I'd glide like the King of Drifters down the coast of Argentina until I was there. I'd never make it, of course. I'd die long before I got there, but that was my best way out. Right now, at this moment, I can't picture Patagonia. All I can think about is Gant and the fact that he's gonna want us dead over this gold."

"How many bullets you got in your gun?"

"Four," Orley said darkly. "And they're twelve years old. I don't know if bullets go stale, but I think I heard they do."

"Well, I was worried before. Now I feel much better." Laney clapped Orley on the back. "Thanks for that."

"My pleasure." Orley rose to his feet. "I'm gonna get my truck in position. I'll walk back an hour before sunrise."

"Don't be late." Laney rose, too.

"I won't. I'll come out of the ravine and see what he shows up with. He's got men with him I'll use my CB and get the highway patrol out here. But that's the last you'll see of me."

Laney watched Orley drunkenly clamber into his truck and drive it across the road, through the low brush, and down into the wide ravine. The headlights submerged below the horizon and a moment later they went out. Laney closed the gate, walked to his truck and took the knife from under the seat. He slipped it into his cowboy boot and went back in the house and sat down on the couch. A little while later he turned out the light, and for a long time he sat in the darkness, staring at the starlit outline of the giant buckle.

9

"Wake up."

Laney opened his eyes. Gant was standing over him with a big, shiny gun in his hand. The gun was pointed at Laney's forehead. He was wearing a white tracksuit and there was a large gold ring on his hairy trigger finger, which somehow struck Laney as more terrifying than the gun itself. Gant was a big man, with a big, hard gut, big hands, and a big bald head that was red with sunburn and flushed with victory.

"Aw shit," Laney whined.

"I found the hole this buckle came out of and followed your tracks to the ring. Idiot." Gant grinned. He had small teeth. "Where's Ralston Orley?"

"Gone." He probably was, too.

"Gone where?" Gant stepped back. "I guess I don't even care. Get up. We're going for a walk."

Laney got to his feet. The door was open on the long light of early morning, maybe half an hour past sunrise. He couldn't believe he'd fallen asleep on the couch. Gant stood aside and gestured with the gun. Laney stepped out and Gant followed.

"Get the shovel from the side of the house," Gant ordered.

Laney did as he was ordered and shot a quick look out at the road. Gant was driving a brand new Cadillac, dark blue this time. There were no passing cars. The morning was clear, cold, and empty. Even the breeze was quiet.

"Let's go see my ring," Gant growled. "After you Bozeman. Don't do anything stupid."

Laney started walking. Gant, he knew, was going to shoot him and bury him in the deep hole the ring was in. He'd drag it out with his car later and then shovel the dirt in on top of him. He was more and more awake as death got closer.

"You don't have to do this, sir. I won't tell a soul."

"I don't believe you." Gant sounded distracted, like he didn't care what Laney said, like he was thinking about something more important, like lunch.

"I can help you," Laney gushed lamely. "I mean, you're gonna need help. Getting the ring outta here."

"No I won't. Stop talking."

Laney walked. He had a hangover, but it wasn't a bad one. He thought about water and shook his head to clear it. "Mr. Gant, before I die you gotta tell me what happened out here."

"No I don't."

Laney was quiet until they got to the ring. It was even bigger than he remembered. A chunk of it was missing from the lip, clearly where Orley had gone at it with a hacksaw during the night. Laney deflated. He was done. He turned slowly and Gant smiled and gestured with the gun.

"Hop down in that hole and look away."

"No!" Laney shouted defiantly. "I won't get into my own grave!"

"Fine." Gant raised the gun and braced himself to fire. Laney raised one hand to shield his face out of reflex and that's when he saw it. His eyes went wide, and Gant noticed and turned to look back.

Ralston Orley stepped forward with his gun raised. His greasy hair was a wild mess, and the side of his face was still wrinkled with the imprint of his truck seat upholstery. He wobbled as he moved, and Laney noted how incredibly bowlegged he was. With a feral grin that showed his big yellow teeth, Orley pulled the trigger. *Click.*

Nothing happened. Orley looked confused, then cursed and threw the gun down. Gant spun to shoot him and right then Laney realized he was still holding the shovel. In one smooth move, he stepped forward and brought the spade around in a whistling arc, straight into the back of Gant's head. Gant dropped to one knee and Laney hit him a second time like he was swinging a hammer, straight down onto the top of Gant's bald head. Gant fell and was still. For a stunned instant, Laney and Orley stared at each other.

"Holy shit," Laney managed.

"I'm gonna hurl," Orley whispered. He reeled and wobbled. "Lordy be."

Laney took Gant's gun and stuck it into the back of his jeans. Gant was breathing like he was asleep, so Laney took the big man's sneakers off and used the laces to tie his hands behind him. Orley watched with a blank expression while he worked. When he was done, Laney blew out a deep breath.

"Help me drag this big bastard back to the house. You get his right leg, I'll get the left."

Orley obeyed without question. Gant was heavy and he left a groove in the rocky hard pack. When they passed the buckle hole, Orley finally spoke.

"Sorry I'm late."

"You were just in time. He was gonna kill me. You saw. That's attempted murder or premeditated manslaughter or something."

"He was gonna kill me too." Orley labored on. "What- what's the plan now."

"We question him at gunpoint, remember?"

"Oh. Right."

"He didn't tell me shit on the walk here. You see anybody else?"

"He came alone." Orley managed a chuckle. "Man is so greedy and paranoid he done screwed himself."

Dragging Gant up the single step was ugly business, but not as ugly as getting him upright and tied to a chair with old rope from the mining equipment display. Orley kept knocking Gant's head around until Laney finally took over and finished the job himself. When they were done, Laney got the water jug out of the refrigerator and drained off a good two inches. Orley took two sips and spit into the sink, then poured himself a shot of whiskey in a coffee cup and downed it.

"That's better." Orley smacked his lips. "Should we wake him up?"

"How?"

"Throw toilet water on him? I dunno."

Laney went outside. It had turned into a fine morning for an interrogation. The sky was clear, and it was on the cool side, tee shirt weather. He took a deep breath. Orley joined him and together they surveyed the future.

"You gonna make coffee first?" Orley asked.

"What happened?" Laney glanced at him. "I mean, what happened to bladders at dawn?"

Orley shrugged. "I got to thinking. Halfway through the night I got a hacksaw outta my toolkit and snuck on over to the ring. Sawed off a piece. When I got back to my truck, I half planned to light out but I was way too drunk to make it so I thought I'd kick back until I sobered up a little. I think all the sneakin' around wore me out, so I dozed off. Woke up and I'll be damned if Gant wasn't already here. I came in hot, but there was nobody in the house, so I knew where you two were headed. You know the rest."

"You're a bad partner, Orley."

"We ain't partners, son. Don't you forget that. I'm gonna need Gant's gun now."

"No."

Laney went back in and started the coffee. Gant was still out when he returned to the porch with two cups. Orley took his and drank with great relish.

"This is full circle," Orley declared. "On this bright, beautiful morning a full circle has formed."

"Orley, man, the peyote you took in 1989 is–"

Orley laughed, a surprising, clean laugh of pure joy. "No son, hear me out. Now, we know that man in there did some bad shit to get where he is. Don't matter that we don't know what it is. He was about to kill you, then he was aimin' at me, so we know what we know about him.

Gold can get a curse on it, you know that. So can diamonds and rubies and whatnot, but gold for sure. Gant's gold is cursed, Laney. S'why he's tied up in that chair right now. Our gold, as in mine and yours, is curse free. S'why we're enjoying this fine morning with this fine coffee." Orley shook his head. "Glory be."

He was right, Laney realized, and he smiled too. "Maybe you are smart enough to change your terrible ways, Orley. If you're smart enough to figure that out, you might be capable of anything."

Orley winked. "Don't count on it."

I O

When Gant opened his eyes, Laney was standing above him with the gun pointed at his forehead, their situations reversed. Orley was beside him, thumbing a kitchen knife and grinning. To Laney's great shame, it was Orley who asked if his cellphone could record. Laney activated the mic as soon as Gant let out his first pitiful moan. They needed a confession if they were to get on with their lives and this was the moment to get it.

"Oh my god," Gant muttered, focusing on them. He tried to rise and discovered he was tied to the chair he was sitting in, hands behind him, properly secured. He didn't bother to struggle and sighed heavily instead, as if he knew this would happen. "You two." He coughed and rolled his neck. "It's the little things, am I right?"

Laney held the old photo out with his free hand. "Who's the dead man in this picture."

"The man you killed, Gant," Orley clarified. "The man who's ring you were fixin' to kill poor Laney for."

"Danny." Gant licked his dry lips. "His name was Danny Mansfield. He was my best friend and I killed him in cold blood. Just think what I'm gonna do to you two." He managed a cold smile. "Unless you kill each other first." His mean chuckle turned into a dry cough.

Laney and Orley looked at each other.

"You killed your best friend?" Laney felt lightheaded.

"I had to. I was in love with his wife Betty. We were having an affair."

Gant's eyes narrowed. "You guys gonna shoot me now? Is that the plan? Bury me out there in lot nine? I have a better idea. Why don't you-"

"The only killer here is you," Laney interrupted quickly. He took his phone out of his breast pocket and showed it to him. "Your confession." He stopped recording and pocketed it. Gant tried for a smile that didn't quite make it this time.

"Lotta good that'll do you. No body, no crime. Only bone I saw had turned to dust centuries ago."

"Missing person, murder confession," Orley countered. "You don't know shit about a damn thing, Gant. This is New Mexico. They'll put you in lockup here just for confusing 'em." He elbowed Laney. "Me and you. Outside."

Laney followed Orley out and away from the house. Orley was surprisingly sober.

"That's good enough for me, son. I'm taking his Caddy and goin' to Ruidoso. I'll trade it to Rudy like I said and come back with the torch, be back before dark if I leave right now."

"What about Gant?"

Orley scowled. "I don't care. I'd probably kill him if it was just me. Man is a murdering wife stealer, and he might even be some kinda sorcerer. You do whatever you want, just don't tell me, I don't want to know. We cut the ring in half tonight, then we go left and right, just like we planned." Orley looked out at the road. "Can't believe it but this idiot plan of ours just might hang together." Then he gave Laney a hard stare. "Don't do anything stupid, boy. Gant says he has to go to the bathroom you tell him to hold it. He stays tied up. Man is dangerous and you're- you're Laney Bozeman."

"Roger that."

Orley already had Gant's keys and his wallet. Without another word, he got in the Cadillac and roared off in a cloud of dust. Laney closed the gate behind him and watched until the car was out of sight. When it was gone, he stared a little longer before he finally looked back at the sun-bleached old bungalow. In theory, they had most of what they needed to keep Gant from hunting them down, but they didn't have all the answers. Laney believed he might get away with his life at this point. He might even get away with some gold. But more than anything he wanted to leave with the truth. He was tired though. Almost being killed in front of his own grave had physically taxed him, and everything seemed too loud and too bright, like he'd just recovered from a tropical fever. The thought of talking to Gant and probing into his stale bummer of a life was almost too much to bear. Laney heaved a heavy sigh and went back into the bungalow.

Gant watched him enter with an expression of unconscious contempt. He either couldn't help himself or it was his resting, natural face. Laney dragged a chair out from the kitchen and sat down across from him. The giant belt buckle took up much of the room, so they were close, close enough for Laney to smell Gant's musky yet subtle cologne.

"I still got questions," Laney began.

Gant cracked a mean smile. "Curiosity killed the cat."

Laney looked down at the floor. He felt like he was hallucinating. Even tied up in a chair, his car freshly stolen, beaten with a shovel, and with his gun in another man's hands, Gant still lorded it up like he was tied to a throne made out of his own cash. On top of everything else, the man was quite possibly crazy.

"Me and Danny were MPs," Gant began, falling with those few words into a storyteller's rhythm. "That's military police. Stationed in Los Alamos, then Alamogordo. We stuck together, Danny and me. Four long years of sitting around in one booth after another, we got to be friends of a sort. After we mustered out, we both went to work for a guy by the name of Kurt Hackensack. Ran a black service called M4Z, private security." Gant stirred a little and Laney watched his eyes grow distant as he sauntered down memory lane. "Hackensack was a regular customer of ours when we were on gate duty. Always came at night and he always seemed like a spook, so when we signed on, we thought we'd see some of the juicy classified stuff we knew he was tangled up in. Turned out to be boring work. Security is dull, but M4Z was something else. Compartments within compartments. We transported things from A to B, and the people we picked up from knew as much as the people we delivered to, which was nothing, so nobody ever knew a damn thing about- anything. It was unreal. In the end, I don't think even Hackensack knew what was going on. All that time, he just liked acting mysterious. But that old boy was way out in the dark with the rest of us."

"I know that feeling," Laney said softly, almost to himself. Gant didn't hear him and continued.

"Me and Betty took up at a Christmas party. Danny was an amateur geologist, always out in his back shed with his precious rocks and his dumbass catalogs. He took night classes when it didn't interfere with work, said he was gonna make something of himself. Betty stuck with him all the years we were in the service, and she kept her head down while we worked for M4Z, doing whatever it was we were doing. But the rocks. That was too much. A woman can't lose out to geology. It just ain't done. I saw my window that Christmas Eve, when everyone at their party finally went home and it was just me and Bets and we found that Danny Boy was gone, off in the shed again with his azurite and his vanadinite. I was in, just like that."

Gant was quiet for a moment. Laney's hangover pulsed, and he took a page from Orley's book and chased it away with a sip of whiskey. Gant didn't even see him move. Laney thought he might be looking back through time at Betty, dressed in her holiday finery all those years ago, having just discovered that her husband left her at a party at their own house.

"She didn't love me, Betty didn't. Not like she loved Danny." It came out cold and factual. "She was lonely and hurt in an unusual way by his interest in gems and rare minerals, and I was interested in her, it was simple as that. At the time, me and Danny were part of a transport and security detail for a little private sector lab outside of Los Alamos. Five cinderblock buildings, didn't even have a name, so we called the facility Five Block. We guarded the perimeter against spiders and tumbleweeds and occasionally we transported unmarked boxes to the base. The eggheads who came and went let enough drop for us to know they were working on radios, which was horse shit and we knew it. Me and Betty carried on all winter, stealing time when Danny was at his night classes. That spring we found even more time when Danny inherited some chump change and bought a worthless patch of desert and built a little bungalow on it. This place. He had big dreams, see." Gant snorted. "Danny wanted to start up a little souvenir junk shop called The Rock Shack."

Laney gulped. It was clear, somehow, that Gant avoided thinking about those days, and he'd certainly never told anyone about them. This was the first time he'd recounted this awful string of thefts to anyone. The confessional nature of it made Laney's hands and feet feel clammy, like he was in a cold movie theater on a hot and swampy day. Still, he couldn't help it when he leaned in a little.

"Years," Gant continued in a quieter, haunted voice. "I spent so many years trying to understand what happened next. Work at the lab was heating up and the geeks thought they were on to something big. Parts were coming and going. Me and Danny pieced it together, mostly Danny, because he found it fascinating. The boys in Five Block were working on remote projection entanglement, they called it. The idea is easy enough to understand. You got a small mind, Laney, which is ironic and even that will be lost on you, but I'll break it down. Take an atom and zap it with a laser. It will shed energy in the form of two electrons. Those electrons are entangled. But the easiest way is to just bring particles together and let them interact, creating a joint superposition. We knew this way before Bell in 1964, he just proved it. The geeks in Five Block, they were trying to create a state of entanglement without any previous interaction. Non-conventional, remotely generated entanglement. And in that reaching out and digging down they found what Einstein called a hidden variable, but not one he would have ever imagined. They tapped into a kind of primordial entanglement that occurred when the universe itself was young and small, at the edge of baryogenesis, when everything that became anything was in one big ball. They discovered the interconnectedness of all things."

"So these guys... they found a connection, like, between everything and... everything else?" Laney had to pee, but he held it.

"They did." Gant's eyes briefly went glassy. "For all the wrong reasons they did."

Laney swallowed. "Reasons are important."

"Me and Betty, we were hot and heavy but there was always that sadness in her, that guilt." Gant was almost talking to himself now. "I couldn't spackle it over. I started to hate Danny because of it. He was so driven, so curious and true. Never late, clean shave every time, guy was a boy scout in a world of jackals, and he didn't even know it. What a rube." Gant licked his dry lips and his beady eyes flared with a malice that had never died. "The boys in Five Block, their sub-stratum primordial entanglement device, was a thing they called The Karikov Projector. They'd remotely entangled an electron in building one with an electron in building five and they were ready to pull the trigger on something way bigger. Tiny sheets of graphene. But something unexpected happened when they did." Gant's eyes glazed over. "The graphene target in building five... it doubled."

Laney was following along as best he could, but this threw him. Gant focused on him for the first time in his telling and grinned a bad grin.

"Those geeks, though. At that point, they did something that made me wonder at the nature of genius. They cranked up the juice and turned that projector on a mouse in building one, just to see what happened." He closed his eyes. "A mouse," he said again. "Just 'cause they were curious."

"Aw man," Laney whispered. "Fuck those guys."

"The first mouse just- vanished. Poof. Gone. No change to the corresponding mouse in building five. They thought it might have been vaporized. When they figured out that wasn't the case they were deeply freaked out, but they were also... scared. But most of all they were fascinated because they set up another mouse and did it again. Then again. And again. Every mouse vanished, and they never figured out what happened to them. Fifteen mice down the line they called it, and by then those guys were... different. They never reported any of it. They did, the bigger geeks in Sandia and White Sands would have taken over and our Five Block boys woulda been out. Danny thought there was more to it than the boys in the lab not wanting to share their toys. No, they believed they'd touched on something we shouldn't be fooling around with. They were scared. They boxed up the Karikov Projector and one lonely morning they tasked me with transporting it all the way to Nellis. It was going into storage. One more gizmo for the warehouses full of secrets better left in the dark."

Laney could see where this was heading. Gant killed Danny with the entanglement mice gun. He glanced at the giant belt buckle, then back at Gant.

"Danny was working on the bungalow that weekend. Betty was at home in Alamogordo, dying of loneliness and sorrow. So I took my shot. I was alone on that detail, so I stopped on by. Danny was out in lot three, rootin' around in the sand. He looked so happy when I pulled up. Waved to me. I went around to the back of the truck, took out the Karikov Projector and pointed it at him and just like that, I popped him. The lab boys, they had to spend hours lining everything up, getting the field depth just right, all the coordinates just perfect, but shit, I clipped into the power supply they boxed up with it, cranked the dial and pulled that trigger. It was a toggle, really. There wasn't even a sound." Gant closed his eyes. "Not even a click. Danny vanished. Just like the mice."

Laney's mouth was hanging open. He closed it.

"After that I went on, just business as usual. Delivered the Projector, signed it off, went home, went to work, rinse and repeat. A few days later Danny was declared missing. Cops asked me a few questions, then a few suits outta White Sands. People figured he'd either run off or got lost way out in the desert by his cabin and died out here, never to be found. I courted Betty even harder, and in her grief, she finally accepted me. For a little while, I was almost happy.

"The boys in Five Block started working on something new and a year passed. One day some construction guys showed up and it turns out they're expanding. Five Block was gonna be Six Block." Gant took a breath. "They were digging for the new foundation when they found the first skeleton. At first, they couldn't figure it out, thought it was a malformed wooly mammoth or a giant sloth. Then they found the head or the tail. It was one of the mice. That night they uncovered five more." Gant's eyes watered. "They were... huge. Giant mice skeletons. Some of the eggheads cracked straight through the middle and had to be quietly carted away that night. Gant gave Laney a hard look.

"Well? What'd they say?"

"I don't think any of them ever really figured it out. One guy said that substratum entanglement exists because everything came from the same thing, that original badass singularity. This other fella- he'd gone super crazy and was raising goats in Utah- he said that everything in that experiment was about vibration. Everything is just a vibration in what he called the density garden. And when you touch the Higgs medium that binds it all, when you put energy into it, you can displace vibrations in spacetime. Hence the mice and Jamison." Gant suddenly seemed mad. His eyes rolled with delight and a delirium touched his features. "I turned Danny into a giant and I booted his ass through time. Danny... he told me once that a day would come when science was indistinguishable from magic. And I turned him into a giant. Me." Gant cackled, a twisted, wracking thing that sounded like Orley's maniacal parrot laugh after they discovered the ring in the photograph. Laney felt nauseous. "I performed that magic when I killed Danny. The line- it blurred right there in my hands. I felt it." Gant's eyes were wide. He took a sharp breath through his nose and snapped out of it, dropping back into reverie. "They figure the giants died on the spot, every last one of them. Asphyxiated because they were made for bigger oxygen or some shit. That accounted for some of the mice having made it a little ways out from building five."

"Jeez."

"Yeah." Gant was quiet for a moment. "Me and Betty married a year later. I quit M4Z and started a dry cleaning business. That's a racket, I tell you what. Turned it into a chain of six and sold it for a fortune. Some fifteen years ago I came across some old photos and that was the first time I noticed Danny's ring. This place was just sitting here, thank god I never found a buyer. So I knew that ring was out here. Just a matter of how far good old Danny made it before he dropped."

"You started The Rock Shack. Danny's dream. And you hired bums to look for him. People nobody would ever miss, looking for a guy who got shot through time so you could..." Laney couldn't finish his summary. His grip tightened on the gun.

"Pretty clever, at least I thought so. Only person who missed Danny was poor Betty. I never did make her happy. She died eleven years ago. After that, I hit the sands out here in earnest. I was gonna see my reward for a life with that sad little woman." Gant laughed bitterly. "She never stopped waiting for that rockhound of hers. She always thought Danny was out there somewhere, maybe doing classified work for M4Z."

Gant stopped talking and stared into the middle distance, lost, somewhere else entirely. Laney watched him for a long time before he said anything.

"Mr. Gant." Laney licked his lips. "You, ah, you're crazy. This whole thing gave you the banana fruit loops."

Gant's eyes glittered when he looked up. "Magic happens all around you every day. You don't know how that TV works. Not really. You don't even know how or why you're alive. Even that's a magical mystery. I made a giant and lost him in the past. Big deal. The past is full of big shit that overshadows the little now. The science or the magic of how things happen doesn't matter. Why it happens doesn't matter, either. The only thing that matters is what comes next."

Laney couldn't take another word of it. He rose and stumbled outside, moving as if through a haze. The day had turned warm. He wanted Orley to come back. Ralston Orley was so much better than the man behind him. He just wanted to talk to him. Talk to anyone, really. Laney scanned the horizon. Even talking to a bird would do. He somehow had to distance himself from what he'd just learned. He took his phone out and looked at it. Nothing from Maria. A single smiley face emoji would have made a world of difference just then. Laney lowered his phone and went back inside.

"You hungry?" he asked Gant. The big man was sweating, lost in thought. He glanced at Laney and cocked his head.

"Whatcha got?"

"Tamales. Got 'em off an old lady outside that little grocery store in Ruidoso."

Gant shook his head. "Not in a million years. But I'd take a hit off that crap whiskey."

Laney picked up the bottle and carefully dumped some into Gant's upturned mouth. He swallowed and sputtered and then shook his head like he'd just dunked his face in ice water.

"Bam! Right in the liver! My first drink in nine years!" Gant licked his lips and gestured with his head. "C'mon. Hit me again. Gimme a double."

Laney obliged. Gant downed a good four fingers of the bottle before he finally pulled back and spluttered. Laney backed away and winced, sure he'd just done the wrong thing. Gant hit him with a hard smile.

"Don't gimme that look, son. I ain't a drunk. I can't drink and take Viagra on the same day and I ain't getting any tonight. Parade rest, soldier."

"Gant," Laney began slowly, "you- you need help man. Like, you need a priest with a degree in psychology or, like, therapeutic Himalayan monk chants and a special helmet. I don't know what you need."

Gant chuckled. "Betty said the same thing."

Laney sat back down. He carefully wiped the mouth of the bottle before he drank.

"Time." Gant was clearly relieved to finally talk. Spilling his guts was so cathartic for him that he seemed smaller, as if the iron rod in his back had softened. "That buckle, that ring, all that gold... it's all tied to the murder of my best friend, entangled with it. My sins, my bad wishes, my malice were projected into it."

"Like smell-o-vision." It came out as a whisper.

"The Karikov Projector was just like a movie projector that way, but it projected my essence, and up until now I've been the only audience. My fate was tied to all this. Now your ambitions have come into the picture, yours and Ralston Orley's. You and that wretched drunk are gonna steal more than my gold." Gant turned his burning eyes on Laney. Even in defeat, he seemed smug and overlarge. "Now we'll see what awful things are inside you two, ready to be made large on the great screen of spacetime."

Laney smiled at that, and the smile felt like a burst of sunlight on his face. Gant snapped back like Laney had touched him with a live wire.

"No more talking, Gant." Laney's smile dropped. "You change your mind about the tamales, you just ask, but that's the only thing I wanna hear from you."

Ralston Orley returned just before sunset. He was driving a rusted, smoking tow truck that sounded like it was a mile away from death when he rumbled through the gate.

"Look at this." Laney slapped the dusty hood of the truck as Orley got out. "This is gonna do it. Got the torch?"

"In back." Orley held up a six pack and a greasy paper bag. "And I got beer and cheeseburgers."

"Damn." Laney accepted a beer and drank thirstily. Orley peered at the house, then cracked a beer of his own.

"Gant spew a bunch of shit while I was gone?"

"Sure did. Crazy as hell."

"Figures."

Laney blew out a breath. "That buckle and the ring, shit, he stole the guy's wife and The Rock Shack too. This place wasn't even his idea. Everything went giant when he shot the poor fella with a classified mice gun. Gant thinks his bad juju got all tangled up in the whole mess, like ear wax in a jug of water."

Orley's eyes widened. "So he's *crazy* crazy."

"Yep. But he ain't as smart as we thought. Gant missed much of what happened to him, or at the very least misinterpreted it. Lust, greed, bad wishes and what have you, that's what he focused on because that's what he understands. But I had all afternoon to think on it and I can see a different pattern beyond that." Laney gestured at the wide world with his beer. "The science guys and Gant had the same motivation, the same crappiness of intent, and their bad juju made a bad thing worse, but when you think about it, the interconnectedness of all things... there's a looping quality to it, a feel of fate to it all, as if time and destiny and the map of reality has an underlying code... Like a great big bingo card... And all the letters are in a different alphabet and yet you still know just from looking that they're letters..." Laney trailed off.

Orley grunted. "His crazy wore off on you, boy."

"Maybe so."

Orley gestured at him with his beer. "Let's focus on reality here, Laney. I don't need more nuts in my sundae."

Laney took the burgers out of the bag and handed one to Orley. He immediately recognized the plain, greasy wrapper. Laney unwrapped his and studied it with great appreciation before he took a bite, then chewed with his eyes closed, savoring it. When he opened them, he discovered Orley eating like he hadn't eaten in weeks.

"Bucky's Burgers," Laney marveled. "How'd you find that little food truck? I thought he had, like, ten customers and I was two of 'em." There were two food trucks in Ruidoso, and Bucky's was the one nobody could ever find. He moved often, and he'd never yet selected a good location.

"Me and Buck go way back," Orley managed. He swallowed a huge bite and then talked around the next one, making a real mess of it. "Worked the state fair circuit together from '85 to, oh, guess it was '88. Best god damn job I ever had. I worked the ring toss, I forget what Buck did, I think he was on the toilet brigade. I tell you what son, them carnies know how to party." Orley raised his burger. "Wouldn't say we're friends, more like fellow drunks, but when he started his little food wagon, I gave him a friendly idea. The green chilis. That was all me."

Laney didn't believe him, but he didn't say anything. They ate in silence after that. A green chili cheeseburger with the right backdrop was a nearly religious experience. When they were done, Orley wiped his hands on his pants and cracked a second beer. Laney used a napkin from the bag. Neither of them were in a hurry to do anything. Eventually, Orley belched and tossed his head at the bungalow.

"I was thinking. Gant? Special kind of fool in there."

"I feel special too."

Orley squinted. "We got nothin' to lose, boy, and he knew it. Any move we make is totally unpredictable because of it, I mean even we don't know what we'll do. We weren't supposed to be able to get along or work together and here we are, drinkin' beer and eatin' deluxe cheeseburgers. We're supposed to be smart enough to figure out how to tie our own shoes and that's about it, but look who's tied up in there with that freakish buckle. And we're supposed to be aimless as can be, but look at us. We both know where we're goin' after this." He sighed. "But most of all, we ain't got no guard rails, me an' you." Orley raised his beer. "No plan at all was the best plan ever, I damn well knew it all along. Look where all that carelessness got us." He grinned and shook his head. "Almost like he wanted this to happen."

Laney smiled. Orley didn't give him time for a rejoinder and instead pointed at the contraption in the back of the tow truck. Most of the torches Laney had seen looked like a spray wand connected to a small battery charger box. This looked like a copper baseball bat fused with a discount espresso machine and connected by dangerous looking exposed wires to the guts of an old fashioned microwave.

"Plasma torch is jerry-rigged half to hell, but it'll do the job. Before I swapped for it I had Rudy cut the end off an old girder segment they were using as a wheel mount. Went through it like a chainsaw through a watermelon. You trust me to do it I'll make the cut while you watch our man in there. When it's done, we roll our trucks over one by one and load 'em up with the tow winch here. Then we all part ways."

"What about the tow truck?"

Orley shrugged. "Leave it. Fact is I think it might be stolen."

"Right on, man." Laney took another beer. "Honk if you need me."

Laney couldn't bear to face Gant again. He peeked in and saw that Gant was lost in thought, staring at the belt buckle, but after that he waited on the porch. A single car drove past, but The Rock Shack wasn't open, and they didn't slow down. An hour passed. Then another. Laney was just about to check on Gant again when in the distance he heard

Orley beep the horn on the tow truck. The ring was cut. Laney checked on Gant and found him dozing, still firmly secure, so he got in his truck and drove slowly over the rocky ground to where Orley worked.

"That was a bitch," Orley reported. He was drenched in sweat and drinking a final beer. "Kinda hot so watch it."

The giant ring was cut in two. Laney stood next to Orley and together they just stared at it.

"Piece on the right looks a tad bigger," Orley said. "I'll take that one since I did all the work."

"Good deal."

"Back your truck up and I'll hoist yours up in the bed."

Laney backed his truck around. Orley roped the left half crescent of gold around the tow joist and worked the gearbox to lift it. Laney backed under it and Orley slowly lowered it into place. Laney took his old blue rain tarp and tucked it around the metal, then used a bungee cord to hold it in place. When he was done, it looked like he was transporting a poorly wrapped tractor rim. There were several splashes of molten gold in the sand that had cooled into odd, flat shapes. Laney picked up three of them and showed them to Orley, who nodded. They were still warm to the touch. Laney pocketed them and got in his truck.

"Move out," Orley said curtly. He hopped in next to him and they rode in silence. Once they were back at the bungalow, Orley disappeared across the road and a moment later Laney heard the sound of Orley's truck engine. He wheeled past a minute later, and ten minutes after that he was back. Orley got out and peered into the bungalow at Gant, then squinted at Laney.

"He's all yours. You decide his time is up make sure to fill in the hole."

Laney nodded. Orley looked west.

"Your donut shop is east of here. I'll go west."

"All right then."

Orley looked across the road. "I kept thinking on my life and times after I dragged that buckle into the living room. That's what happened to me, Laney. I wasn't so much in a blackout drunk as I was in shock at the impossible. People say that when you think you're gonna die your life flashes before your eyes, and I know that to be true. I been there. That night with the lightning woman for instance. But when- when you see a small miracle or a thing that shouldn't be- pretty much the same thing- for me it was like that near death flash, but I could see a thousand roads I might have taken and a thousand I still might." Orley shook his grizzled head. "Boy, you know, in my whole damn life I never really tried hard at a damn thing. But that's over. Don't know about you, but I'm gonna do it right from here on out." He nodded. "I'm gonna really wreck some shit."

Laney nodded. Orley didn't try to shake hands. The boozy old shoveler got into his truck and rolled out onto the road. He left the gate open, and without a backward glance, he headed west, blasting into the sunset. Laney watched until he was out of sight and then he just stood there. He'd seen countless New Mexico sunsets, but for some reason, this was the first time he really looked as far as he could into one. The scattered clouds were lit from below with flaming tangerine and sour lemon candy yellow, and that gave way to the cool gray body the color of whales in a cold sea, and above that sleeping blue, the same shade as the morning glories under the window of a house he could barely remember. The sky itself was huge, so vast that it forced a filling quiet into the world beneath it. His bones, Laney realized, had been resonating with the emptiness of this place all along. In a trance, he turned and went back inside one last time.

"I ain't gonna kill you." It came out of Laney in a halting voice, as if he'd just woken up. Gant was still looking at the buckle. The smugness, the righteous greatness that emanated from him earlier was gone, replaced with a strange vulnerability. He focused on Laney and smiled sadly, then tossed his head at the giant buckle.

"This buckle is mine."

Laney nodded, surprised. "Sure man. You can have it, totally all you."

"No, I mean I just realized it's mine, as in I own it. I'm sure of it. I left that belt at Betty's. I don't think Danny ever even knew it was mine. If he did, I wonder now if he was trying to send me a message of some kind, waiting for me to notice, thinking it was a way to tell me he knew what I was up to."

Laney took the hunting knife from his boot and showed it to Gant. He dropped it, point down, and it stuck in the scarred floor.

"I'm leaving that for you, Mr. Gant. You tip that chair over, sort of worm along and you can get your hands on it and cut yourself loose. I bet that takes you an hour or two. There's a piece of shit tow truck parked out there somewhere, or you can wait and thumb a ride. Landline still works in case you got a single friend in the world you can call for help." Laney drew Gant's gun and showed it to him. "Leading cause of death for gun owners is a bullet from their own piece, and that's gonna be you if I see you again. I even suspect you're lookin' for me or Ralston Orley and I'll turn your confession over to the military in White Sands. Those guys are scary, and I bet they'd be real interested in you."

Gant stared at him, as if he didn't understand at all. Laney cleared his throat and gave him a pained, even embarrassed smile.

"Orley, he, ah, he wanted me to give you a message, too." Laney looked down and shuffled his feet. "I promised him so here it is. Seems Ralston Orley met a few shady characters on his way between here and there. You know him. He's, well..." Laney looked up. "He says he knows some guys that nobody would ever want to know. First thing he's gonna do is give those bad men some cash and your name. He ever disappears, you do too. Maybe he's bluffing." Laney shrugged. Gant looked deflated, but in a minor way, like he was listening to elevator music while eating something bland. His high horse had run out from underneath him and vanished over the horizon.

"You win, Bozeman." Gant shook his head and looked at the buckle again. Laney did, too. It was even worse now, pitted and ancient still, but now tangled through time with Gant's darkness. "Congratulations, son. My curse is all yours. You're welcome to it." He really believed it, too.

"You know," Laney said slowly, "this could have shaken out differently, Mr. Gant. You'd been an okay guy we would have settled on a thank you and a bonus. But we knew you'd try to kill us and you did. We gave you any of this gold you'd use it to fund a hunt to get the rest. You tied our hands, man. Now you don't get anything."

"I'm free of the tangle," Gant said softly. "I get that. You don't understand right now. But you will."

Gant didn't look back up when Laney left, and Laney didn't look back, either. He even left the gate open. The truck handled differently with such a massive weight in the bed, so he took it slow and steady as he headed west. Ten miles passed before he turned on the radio. The only station he could get was playing mariachi music, which always sounded cheerful to him. After the second tune, Laney rolled his window down and threw Gant's gun into an arroyo.

Selling gold simply wasn't going to be any fun at all no matter how he looked at it. Two hours past the brilliant orange and lavender sunset, Laney pulled onto a side road and stopped. After inspecting one of the gold droppings from the cut, he got out and took a hammer and an old wedge from his toolkit. Working by the dim glow of the taillights, he hammered the smallest oblong little disk into a roundish wad that might pass for something other than melt tailings. When he was finally satisfied, he checked the wrapping on the ring segment and rumbled east again.

He pulled into Ruidoso just after midnight. He had fourteen dollars in cash and almost fifty in his bank account, enough for a cheap motel, but he slept in the truck. At sunrise, he got coffee at a gas station and put twenty bucks in the tank, and then he waited in the parking lot until Fernando's Pawn & Jewelry opened. A man who might have been Fernando himself weighed the gold wad, eyed Laney suspiciously, weighed it a second time, did something with a dropper and some cloth, and in the end gave him three hundred dollars, more than Laney thought he would get but a fraction of what it was actually worth.

From there he headed east to Roswell and Big Donut. The drive normally took him an hour and a half, but he drove slower than usual, taking his time, deep in thought. So many strange things had happened in the history of New Mexico. So many secrets lay within an hour of wherever you were, no matter where you were in the state. The Manhattan Project, the aliens in 1947, that was just scratching the surface, he knew. Guys like Gant worked on secret things they never even understood or knew all that much about, so even the people who made the secrets didn't know most of them. As he drove, Laney thought of his own secrets and how they'd grown in number. Nobody knew he was driving toward a donut shop with a fortune in the bed of his truck. Beyond that, and bigger still, was the newness of the road itself. A slightly different Laney Bozeman was on his way to a different ocean of possibilities, and he'd never tell a soul about that change. The whole thing struck him as too big for his hat size.

Big Donut was just as he remembered it. He'd only been away for a few days, but it seemed like he hadn't seen the place in a long, long time. Maria waved at him from the window, surprised and delighted. She hadn't been expecting to see him for two weeks. Laney straightened his hair.

"Hey Laney!" Maria chirped as he entered. "You get off early?"

"No ma'am." Laney smiled shyly and ran a hand through his hair. "I got fired."

11

Laney Bozeman never saw Mr. Gant or Ralston Orley again. Five years later he drove by The Rock Shack and it had burned to the ground long ago. A few weathered, blacked boards and rusted gears from the mining display were all that remained. He heard a rumor in a bar one night, a fable almost, about a strange man who started a traveling carnival with games and showgirls, full of light and glitter and colored smoke, and paid for it with gold, then drank it all away in a spectacular blaze of glory and vanished into the night. The guy who told him about it had a singular smile on his face, like he'd seen a magnificent but dangerous thing, like a rampaging unicorn or a bejeweled hyena. Laney assumed if it was true that it was Ralston Orley, and he wondered if the old shoveler finally made it to Patagonia with the last of his fortune. Laney was somehow certain he did, and that Orley was there now, wetting an unbaited line in a faraway river and never catching a thing, and in the long evenings he'd tell the mystified local bar patrons, none of whom spoke a word of English, about the time he found a giant belt buckle in the deserts of New Mexico.

As for Laney Bozeman, for want of anything better to do, he started a grocery store, just like he said he would. It didn't work out with Maria Ortiz, but the grocery store did fine. It turned out he needed six of them to launder the money from the gold. Seven, or even ten, would have been better, but after he met Lola Trujillo and got married, he slowed down the expansion to make time for family. It took a decade, but the six stores in the Laney's Grocery line transformed the culinary and nutritional landscape of rural New Mexico. The produce was fresh and the bulk dry goods were of the organic variety. There were Rocky Mountain Basque sheep's milk cheeses and Santa Fe stiltons and Mesquite smoked goudas from Taos, and the tortillas, the donuts, and even some of the breads were made in-house. The splendid deli counters did lively business from opening to closing seven days a week. All six sold good beer and they even had glass bottle wine. Laney bought locally when he could and nearby when he couldn't, and he encouraged tamale vendors to set up out front at every location.

The many, many people who worked for him really liked working there and it showed. They didn't wear uniforms, just name tags, and all of them called him Laney or sometimes just 'Hey dude'. Laney didn't mind at all.

Acknowledgments

Years ago, my pal Chico and I rented a car and drove from Portland, Oregon to Roswell, New Mexico. We wanted to see the UFO museum and maybe take a poke around the crash site itself. There was whiskey involved in this decision. We went the next day, and we never did any investigating, but we saw the museum, ate some great food, and explored New Mexico, a state I'd barely escaped once years before as a fugitive runaway teen. It was January and we had a few storms to outrun, and while we were inadvisably speeding along under the leading edge of a biblical bummer of black cloud, way out there west of Ruidoso... That's where I got the idea for I Shop At Laney's. I thought about the many connections between the very small and the very large and how they might be refined into a single ghostly thread that ran through everything, everywhere, always. The outline migrated from napkin to notebook to computer. I lost it and found it again a few times. A short story version I never dialed in came and went, and short stories don't pay for shit so... And then one night about a year ago, right as I was falling asleep, the ghost thread solution came to me. All I needed, all along, was a giant belt buckle and a grocery store. Special thanks to Brian 'Chico' Joseph, Mikel Ross, Nick Yetto, David Massar, Derek Douglass, KW Jeter, Robert Burg of The Lost Fisherman in Albuquerque, Vincent Kelso, Ph.D., my in-laws Richard and Ellen Mann, and my lovely and talented wife Sylvia. Thanks also to the great state of New Mexico, it really is a special place, and a very special thanks to all at Radio Lake,